Denton Jaques Snider

Agamemnon's Daughter

Denton Jaques Snider

Agamemnon's Daughter

ISBN/EAN: 9783337243449

Printed in Europe, USA, Canada, Australia, Japan

Cover: Foto ©Andreas Hilbeck / pixelio.de

More available books at **www.hansebooks.com**

AGAMEMNON'S DAUGHTER.

An Epopee

BY

DENTON J. SNIDER.

NEW EDITION.

ST. LOUIS.
SIGMA PUBLISHING CO.,
210 PINE STREET.
1892.

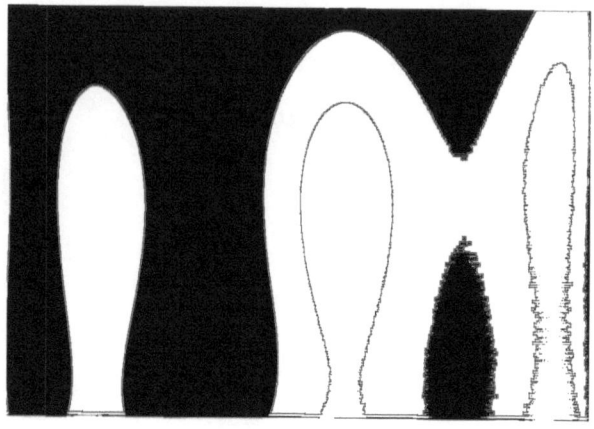

Press of Nixon-Jones Printing Co.

CONTENTS.

Inscribed

To mine own only daughter, still young, but old enough to be deeply sympathetic with this story of Agamemnon's daughter, and often recalled, between lines, in strong compassion for the father by the

Father.

February, 1885.

Canto First.

Iphigenia at Mycenæ.

Innocence and Guilt.

ARGUMENT.

The scene of the legend of Iphigenia at Mycenæ is laid in the city of Mycenæ; the incidents transpire before the Trojan War, and before the abduction of Helen, though they lead up to the latter event. The story has two main points: the visit of Paris from Troy and the visit of Helen from Sparta, into both of which visits the tale of Iphigenia is woven.

I. Paris arrives and is received by the king, Agamemnon, who has the ambition of uniting the European and Asiatic branches of the great Hellenic people. Both Greeks and Trojans are Hellenes (pronounced as two syllables in English), the one with an Occidental, the other with an Oriental tendency.

By giving his daughter Iphigenia in marriage to Paris, Agamemnon hopes to accomplish his plan. But the bard, who feels the inherent antagonism of the two sides, opposes the plan, and tells his dream, which prefigures the grand conflict of the future. Iphigenia, the daughter, opposes also, and will have nothing to do with Paris. She quits his presence, and secretly goes to the fane of Artemis, the Goddess of virgin purity, which is in a retired spot on the mountain above the city. There she receives from the Goddess the message

(6)

which announces the whole circle of her life— her sacrifice, her rescue, her mission to Barbary, her return to Hellas.

Meanwhile Mycenæ is having a merry time in entertaining Paris, who charms all, both men and women. But there is one of his company, Antenorides, who feels and foretells what is coming. (I.—LII.)

II. In the midst of the entertainment Helen arrives from Sparta to take part in the festival. The most beautiful woman of the land is received by the King and the Greeks with great honor and admiration. Iphigenia comes from the shrine of Artemis and meets Helen, who recognizes in the maid a higher nature than her own, and receives from her a token. But soon Helen sees Paris, who, after the song in her praise by the bard, the voice of Greece, meets her and bids her follow him to Troy. At first she yields; then, coming upon Iphigenia, she masters her fateful passion, and starts for home the next morning early. But she still thinks of Paris, and on the way she enters the temple of Aphrodite, who bids her follow Paris, when a violent storm arises through which she flees to Sparta.

The people of Mycenæ know not what to make of her sudden flight. Paris at once sets out for home in pretense, but for Sparta in reality, though under protest of Antenorides. A messenger rides into Mycenæ and announces the flight of Helen; then Menelaus himself arrives. The note of war is heard through Hellas. (LIII. to the end.)

I.

O what is this which sings within the mind,
　As round the land of Hellas fair I tread!
O what is this which always I can find
　Alive and speaking still, though long since dead,
　Still present to mine eyes, though it be fled
Thousands of years in its Hellenic glory!
　An ancient tale to modern music wed —
Hear now the rhyme and hearken to the story.

II.

It was a golden day around the towers
　Of rich Mycenæ with her crown of stone;
The Spring danced up the hill with lap of flowers,
　Which she through all the blooming plain had
　　strown;
　The fragrant Wind did flute his sweetest tone
Amid the bending branches of the tree;
　On every grassy plot Love built a throne,
The time was full of Heaven's minstrelsy.

(9).

III.

The city had a hill within its wall —
  And still it may be seen, a towering crest —
Which from its tireless watch looked down on all,
  At times like war's fierce eagle from its nest,
  At times the hilltop heaved as if the breast
It rose in swift response to tender eyes,
  With gentle breath of poesy caressed;
To-day it swells to soft blue Grecian skies.

IV.

Around the maiden city's swelling breast
  Was drawn a wall, a moveless rocky band,
Whose heavy clasp her heart within had pressed,
  Without had kept each wanton, lustful band;
  Still every breeze strewed kisses through the
    land,
And tender speechless missives on their way
  Fell down the air, by Aphrodite fanned,
And all declared it was a golden day.

V.

Then broke upon the sight a pageant new
  Across the grainfields by the sunlit sea,
Where many a sail swan-winged o'er the blue
  Far-quivering main was floating airily;
  That pageant soon a troop was seen to be,
Swimming upon the golden stream of morn;
  A youthful troop of argent chivalry,
With blazons strange bedight and Orient-born.

VI.

Paris of Troy the foremost lording hight,
  The fairest youth of all the Trojan land,
Within his face he bore a sunrise bright,
  The curls danced round his neck in many a
    strand,
A feathery touch slept in his tender hand,
Love's smiles played from his lips into his eye
  Which coldly thence its charmed object scanned :
He sang to harp sweet strains of poesy.

VII.

And with him many Trojan gallants came
  With lightsome heads and lively hearts, save one
Who Antenorides was called by name,
  Of noble father the still nobler son;
He left in Troy a maid whom he had won,
Who unto him, as he to her, was true;
  But his great love could never sadness shun,
For his deep soul presaged the day of rue.

VIII.

The town came forth to see that troop of kings,
  In shining pomp and grand festivity;
The altars smoked with fragrant offerings,
  And through the streets processions moved in
    glee,
Chariots dashed down the hill into the lea,
The merry stream poured out the Lions' Gate,
  Thrown open was old Atreus' treasury,
And ancient fanes shone forth in golden state.

IX.

King Agamemnon moved with gracious cheer,
    He was a lordly man, not old, not young ;
His word was always musical to hear,
        A gold-bossed scepter in his hand he swung,
        While honeyed speech dropped from his fluent
            tongue :
" Pour out thy heart with us, O noble guest,
    This stay of thine shall not remain unsung;
Not all of ours be thine, but all our best.

X.

" Thy glorious name before thee crossed the sea,
    Thy gracious form, the sweetness of thy word;
Friends with the Trojan folk I fain would be,
        And knit a bond whereof no soul has heard;
        Deep in my heart to-day I am bestirred
To break the barrier of yon blue salt flood;
        See there! above us wheels the favoring bird
To join all Hellenes in one brotherhood."

XI.

A look he cast upon his daughter fair,
    Iphigenia, stainless at his side;
The moment Paris bent his glances there,
        She hung her head, her eyes to earth she tied,
        The stranger's look she could not well abide ;
She turned away and hurried through the crowd,
        For in some secret nook she thought to hide,
Far from the festival and tumult loud.

XII.

Back of the court she had a garden seat,
  Where she had nourished many a loving flower;
These were her friends whom daily she would meet
  To hold mute converse for the passing hour,
And over them she held a gentle power;
Oft would they seem to bloom her future ways,
  Of pain and gain foreshow the fitful shower,
The silent destiny in fairest days.

XIII.

To his high palace Agamemnon sped,
  He set before his guests a banquet rare,
The wine soon flashed each face with sunsets red,
  The courtly tongues were cloyed with dainty
    fare;
Many an Argive chieftain too was there,
Out high-hilled cities of the land they came,
  And mingled with the Trojans killing care,
And much they honored the great Prince's name.

XIV.

Paris led off in festive merriment,
  His Trojans well the beaded cup could tease;
Their song of wine with that of women blent
  Revealed the heart in all its hid degrees;
But other strains heard Antenorides,
As he looked on and that mad revel saw;
  For in the wine he could behold the lees,
And could in license read avenging law.

XV.

Yet one relief he had of suffering,
  A single bliss in Hellas he could find,
It was to see the daughter of the king ;
  She raised to life within his boding mind
  The image of the Love he left behind,
And darted through him gleams of happiness
  For one sweet hour; but then again he pined,
And saw his lady pallid in distress.

XVI.

A bard there was who in the palace sang,
  An aged holy man who much had seen ;
Of sorrow he had known the deepest pang,
  Of joy had felt the finest rapture, keen
  Within his soul full strung; at Thebes had been
Twice with the seven Argive chiefs, who sought
  By the pure fire to make that city clean
Of its old fateful taint from Asia brought.

XVII.

Defeat and victory had been his life,
  Once he had lost at Thebes his chieftains all ;
Then he beheld renewed the deadly strife,
  And the proud town one heap of ashes fall.
  Of changeful destiny he was the thrall,
His heart became a harp of many strings,
  Which Fate would strike to make her madrigal,
Whence sparkles fell of all melodious things.

XVIII.

The Muses gave to him a voice divine
  The famous deed heroical to sing;
He hymned his Grecian soul in every line —
  That soul the world to harmony could bring,
  And see its image in the smallest thing ;
But what his people felt, he saw with eyes,
  He flew before them high on eagle's wing,
Discerned the speck across the farthest skies.

XIX.

He felt the struggle coming on afar,
  The burden of his song was Zeus's hest ;
He knew that in the Trojan lay the war
  Which Greek must end by voyages unblest,
  And by a ten years' time of wild unrest ;
That bard — he was a man born into all,
  His glance he threw beyond the mountain crest,
Where he the Future saw and heard it call.

XX.

To Agamemnon now these words he spake ;
  " I bear to thee my heavy soul, O king ;
To-day I fear thou wilt thyself unmake,
  Thy mind soars up beyond all reckoning ;
  Across the seas thy thought has taken wing,
While one now walks thy court in silent quest
  The jewel of our Greece to Troy to bring ;
That man beware, beware the fateful guest.

XXI.

" I saw him in my dazzled dream last night
    Fulfill the perfect circle of his deed;
What is already done, was but a mite,
    A little point flashed with a burning glede;
    More swiftly ran the point than any steed
As it sped round to what was next to be ;
    The Future slid into my vision, freed
From that dark line which is Time's boundary.

XXII.

" High over Troy that point a blaze became,
    It lit and flared on Paris' swollen sail,
The raging Hellespont upsprang in flame,
    Outburning all Jove's lightning and the gale;
    Into Mycenæ swept the fiery trail,
Then back it streamed with tenfold passion dire;
    The sea-foam, Aphrodite's mother pale,
Flamed round the ship and set the waves on fire.

XXIII.

" In his returning ship I saw to be
    What brings to sons of men the most delight,
The highest prize of lofty minstrelsy,
    The soul that thrills into the sense of sight,
    The look that suns the world in newer light;
Then many warriors follow on the wave,
    They fill a plain and soon begin a fight
The stolen prize of their own land to save."

XXIV.

To him replies then Agamemnon proud:
" Great now in Hellas is my sovereign power!
Of men to serve I cannot count the crowd,
  Of islands of the sea I have the flower,
  Beneath this scepter wild Arcadians cower,
The Isthmus links two mighty seas for me,
  Two continents it joins in one high tower
Which shows me forth to rule all Barbary.

XXV.

" But now I bend my look across the sea,
  This day to Asia I shall reach my hand,
And of Troy's citadel the taker be,
  And towns and fields to farthest Phrygian land,
  By that which I have in my bosom planned;
To Priam's son I shall my daughter wed,
  Troy and Mycenæ shall together stand,
Or shall together lie with cities dead."

XXVI.

Forthright the father sought that garden spot,
  His daughter's mind in gentle wise to test,
He found her deep within a darksome grot,
  Where but a single sunbeam, doubly blest
  Played down her forehead and her lips caressed :
" Why hast thou fled away beyond my call?
  Fill up the festal day with thy full zest,
Prince Paris now awaits thee in the hall."

XXVII.

The maiden suddenly became a prayer ;
   Upon the world she gazed with deep blue eyes,
Wherein it melted to a vision fair,
     And rose with music sweet unto the skies,
     As earth might turn a sudden Paradise ;
It was her gift to change the small and bad,
     Till both to boundless good together rise ;
Yet in her glance a suffering she had.

XXVIII.

Of the rich summer time she was the flower
   That dwells beside the wild, far-flashing sea ;
To look beyond she had a subtle power,
     A gleam she threw into infinity
     And there another world could plainly see ;
Mirrored the man she saw in every motion,
     Born in her glance was all he was to be,
His hidden genius on its hidden ocean.

XXIX.

Gentle the maiden spoke her word, but strong :
   " The stranger who has come from Troy to-
     day —
Father, I would not do him any wrong,
     But when I think of him, I cannot pray
     To purest Artemis who is my stay ;
His glances light the air but to cajole,
     To heart he never will a heart repay,
I cannot think he loves one human soul."

XXX.

The father quenched his angry flash, and smiled:
" Oh let no more the winds foreboding sigh
Through all thy young and sunny days, my child !
Let minutes now be mad, and wildly fly
Round thee and Paris mid our revelry.
Not often such a day shines on our towers!
The ancient Sun upon our stones doth lie,
And pours the city full of golden hours."

XXXI.

He turned because he heard the trumpet's blare
Hurrying to his ear leap after leap,
As if a war steed galloped through the air,
Bearing a message o'er a mountain steep,
To rouse the soldier on his guard asleep ;
The King in haste turned back to find his guest,
But he could catch a word that he should keep,
A woeful word torn out his daughter's breast ;

XXXII.

"I feel my foe has come and I shall reap
The harvest ripe which he this day will sow ;
For deed of his I long shall have to weep,
As Ida's maids now melt the mountain snow
With tears for his deep wrongs; I shall not go
With him to Troy; oh let me die forlorn
In Greece ! To me and mine he is the foe,
And him I feel the foe to Time unborn."

XXXIII.

There stands high up above the town a fane
  Whose marble front peeps out the thicket green,
And every stone a softened tint hath ta'en
  Purer than any pearl was ever seen
  Washed in the waters of an ocean clean;
The leaflets flutter noiseless round the side,
  The tree-tops to the roof do fondly lean,
The jewel of the wood within to hide.

XXXIV.

The timid deer sports there without alarm,
  The wary bird need there no trapper fear,
It was a spot where man dared do no harm,
  Peace reigneth in that wood for all the year,
  The fountain's modest joy one scarce will hear,
As it wells out beneath a root of might,
  And trails in crystal pure a leaflet sere,
Or paints a tender stain on pebble white.

XXXV.

In secret soon the maiden thither fled,
  She wound with the transparent happy rill,
That to the fane up in the greenwood led,
  Along a channel sweet with many a trill,
  Whereby she moved through music up the hill;
A pretty fawn she saw within a grot
  To slake its thirst beside the forest still,
Then pass before her to the sacred spot.

XXXVI.

It was a pretty dappled timid thing
    That trembled to its silvery spots of hair,
Then faded from the margent of the spring,
    As if it saw within the waters there
    Some ugly image of a brutish bear;
But as it fled, it ran into a cloud
    Whence flowed soft strains upon the forest air,
Of flute and song mid rustling of a crowd.

XXXVII.

At once broke out of music to the glance
    Bright wreaths of maidens floating in the breeze,
And to the strain they soon began a dance
    Upon the vacant air and through the trees;
    But scarce the eye their fleeting shapes could
        seize,
Until they wheeled above the secret fane;
    Hovering down the sky they dropped with ease,
While to a distant lull had died the strain.

XXXVIII.

This was the home of Dian, these her woods
    Where oft the Goddess rested from the chase,
When she amid the sylvan solitudes
    Had led her choir in the tumultuous race
    And of that sport the air long felt the trace,
Though the gay rout had faded all away;
    It was the soft worn heart's own resting place,
Far from the town, and the bold stare of day.

XXXIX.

A billowy moon-tipped play of fold on fold
  Waved through the middle of that multitude ;
The wreath was broke, and one might then behold
  A form that stepped into the fane and stood,
  While all the train of Nymphs fled through the
    wood,
Some to delight in oaks and some in water ;
  Then spake the queen of that sweet sisterhood
In fond low tones to Agamemnon's daughter :

XL.

" Beware the handsome man within thy walls !
  His eyes' soft sunbeams are a sea of ill,
Within his slippery words lie many falls
  For those who touch the circle of his will ;
  Float not upon the raptured waves that thrill
Out of his being, by Aphrodite's breath
  Stirred to a frenzy that the world shall fill,
And sweep the woman with the man to death.

XLI.

" Thee have I chosen for another deed,
  Thou art to be the vase of suffering ;
The Trojan love shall never be thy meed,
  But a new love thy life to light will bring ;
  And yet thou too wilt not escape the sting
Which the high Gods in greatest deeds bestow ;
  For lands, for worlds thou art the offering,
But I shall save thee at the last sharp blow.

XLII.

" And I shall bear thee to a foreign land,
   Where thou a holy priestess art to be
Within my temple on the wild sea's strand,
   Where broods a world of slavish savagery,
   Which is, by deed of thine, to be made free.
This is the Love which now in thee hath gleamed,
   And not before thou hast brought liberty
Unto that land, art thou thyself redeemed.

XLIII.

" O virgin, I am Artemis, the Queen,
   I roam the wood, I ramble in the sky;
My silver bow hung there thou oft hast seen,
   Illuming night with modest purity;
   To thee of all mankind I feel most nigh,
Upon my path in Heaven the brightest star
   Is thine, dispensing light to Barbary;
Go forth and softly shine with me afar.

XLIV.

" After long years to this old home of thine,
   The Hellas new, thou shalt in joy return;
My brother Phœbus calls thee to his shrine,
   Where thou shalt teach the world what it must
      learn —
   A duty new in living to discern;
By thee, his seeress, shall his fane be trod,
   A higher priesthood shall thy exile earn,
Thou art to be the voice of wisdom's God.

XLV.

" There on old rocky Pytho's deep-cleft crest
   In light thou shalt sit down with speech re-
      newed,
When the great war is over, and holy rest
   Settles upon the land in golden mood
   Of sun and song and blissful plenitude ;
The far Barbarian's love, aye and his sword
   'Tis thine to bring to Hellas for her good;
Restoring her, thou art thyself restored.''

XLVI.

The Goddess vanished from the maiden's look,
   But left her in the glimmer of a dawn
Through which did faint away the tuneful brook,
   And through whose milky haze she saw the fawn
Dart trembling from the wood across a lawn,
   By men pursued with axes flashing bright,
   Till in the rosy distance it was gone
Behind the hills, whence shot anew the light.

XLVII.

There long she stayed, nor did her people know
   Whither the maid this merry while had fled;
Meantime Mycenæ had an overflow
   Of earth below and heaven overhead,
   Of wine and sunshine which all golden shed
Upon that happy feast their richest showers,
   And lightly mid the throng the Muses led
And lulled to rest the swifty-stepping Hours.

XLVIII.

It was time of sweet forgetfulness,
    When Lethe hands to men her deepest draught,
For which full pay she asks — a fierce distress
    When they awake and feel the poisoned shaft,
    Whereof there is no cure in human craft,
But in hot blood-drops gurgling from war's blow,
    When Furies have upon the nations laughed
Their diabolic scorn and overthrow.

XLIX.

Ah yes, it was a merry cheery day,
    Paris the gallant Trojan conquered all,
His Asian tongue could lisp a Grecian lay,
    And sweetest accents mingle in its fall;
    E'en proud Queen Clytemnestra was a thrall
Of that soft spell which men were forced to own:
    He made the people whisper, great and small,
"Lo! he has stolen Aphrodite's zone."

L.

Each minstrel sought to sing his bravest song
    Of heroes great and the heroic deed;
Of war between the Gods and Giants strong,
    Of captive maid by doughty warrior freed,
    Of hearts that must with all men's sorrow bleed,
Of Theseus bold, of suffering Hercules
    Who hath of heroes won the golden meed,
As he who can endure until himself he frees.

LI.

But the one song that people heard above
  All others sung upon that fatal day
With maddest sting — it was the song of love.
  From every street uprose the dulcet lay,
  Tingling the blood to fancy's tricksy play,
And hymning viewless nets by Eros wove,
  Which tangled mortals in the fateful fray
And caught the highest God, old father Jove.

LII.

O Antenorides, what silence deep
  Broods over thee amid the festival!
He marked a moving eye that knew no sleep,
  He heard Cassandra's far forewarning call
  Through revel moan like distant waterfall;
Many a ghostly shape before him stood,
  And drew a bloody sign upon the wall
Mid whisperings low: It cannot come to good.

LIII.

But look beyond, there comes a distant train
  Slow-winding o'er the blue Arcadian hills,
Like a sea-serpent of the richest stain
  It swims and every heart with beauty thrills,
  Yet with prophetic flashings of its ills;
It rears its crest above the verdant height,
  The little vales with lambent streak it fills,
Swimming the landwaves green into the sight.

LIV.

In gorgeous curves rolled on the beauteous thing,
  As it unfolded in the haze of afternoon,
And sweet delirious currents it did bring
  Into the eye, and make the daylight swoon
  Away to dreamy glimmers of the moon ;
But in the sky above there hung a frown,
  A cloud that made a dismal threat, but soon
That cloud had melted to a golden crown.

LV.

'Twas Helen coming up from Lacedemon,
  In bright Mycenæ's joy awhile to stay,
And see the festival of Agamemnon,
  The song, the dance, and the procession gay
  With the sweet bloom of manhood in its May;
Iphigenia too she longed to see,
  Both women live together in my lay,
Twinned deep in storied old calamity.

LVI.

But now she comes, the glorious Spartan Helen,
  Into the Argive plain she bursts like day,
And with her a new world for men to dwell in,
  Life, weary theme, becomes a happy play,
  To Gods serene is turned the human clay,
Of an Elysian change she hath the power,
  Beneath her glance each tree throws out a
    spray,
And where she treads, the earth sends up a
  flower.

LVII.

She moves to Lions' Gate the fairest woman;
  The stony Lions' Heads peep out their lair
Above the rock-built portal, with traces human
  Of Love's sweet trouble for that being rare,
  Whom they within the walls will guard with
      care
As they the city guard and its wise laws;
  To glances soft drops down their savage glare
And tender-hearted grow ferocious claws.

LVIII.

The people line her way along the street,
  The heroes bold take on an humble air,
And in their hearts adore that shape complete;
  The children stand in little groups and stare,
  Wishing that they had Helen's golden hair,
Or hand, or her white robe of fold on fold;
  Even the women must pronounce her fair,
When they her failings all had scanned and told.

LIX.

Within the walls there stands a palace high,
  Whose court is girt with many columns white,
And there the silver fountains gaily ply
  The fragrant air with jets of crystal bright,
  Or send along the sand swift streams of light,
Wreathing around the feet of boys of stone,
  Who hold their torches in the eye of night,
Or lean beside a kingly carven throne.

LX.

Those graven boys will stir from spot to spot,
　They have a life within their marble breast,
For ever fixed in motion in their lot,
　Forever moved by passion is their rest ;
　So has their Maker on their form impressed,
With heart-beats all his own a double soul,
　Which he himself in struggle long possessed,
Ere he could make the warring twain one whole.

LXI.

Beneath a chiseled shape of youthful maid,
　Who coyly touched with dainty finger tip
Her own chaste bosom, full of thoughts unsaid
　Of that sweet hour which brings the lip to lip,
　From whose deep rubied flower lovers sip
Busy as bees — there Helen sat in state ;
　Into all Grecian hearts her glances slip
Never to be forgotten — it is their fate.

LXII.

She greets the thronging heroes one by one ;
　Lord Agamemnon speaks the golden word :
" Hail, Helen, coming like the singing Sun ;
　Through thee what lies within us dark or blurred
　Breaks out the brightest strain that time hath
　　heard ;
That look of thine shall be forever ours,
　And thine our hearts, for thee to battle stirred :
Hear while we swear it, ye Olympian Powers."

LXIII.

All shouted loud applause, the oath they swore,
  Heard by the Gods above in council deep,
Who then resolved the casket to outpour,
  Which, full of evils, they beside them keep
  For man, lest he in sloth may fall asleep,
Or may for fateful deed unpunished go;
  Whereby the innocent must ever weep,
Yoked with the guilty in the chain of woe.

LXIV.

Meantime from Dian's fane within the wood
  The maiden Iphigenia homeward sped,
And soon beside the restless brook she stood
  Which leaps beneath the towers to its bed;
  Many a thought was whirling through her head
Of that strange life of hers which was to be;
  The bodeful words the Goddess to her said,
Fell cascades dark down to a sunlit sea.

LXV.

She passed within the court where Helen stood,
  Who spake a tender greeting as she came;
" Sweet maid! thou hast upon thy face a mood
  Which calls the faithless world by a new name;
  Before thee I confess I feel a shame
That I cannot attain to what thou art;
  How gladly would I change for thee my fame,
And in my life feel full thy steadfast heart!

LXVI.

" Deep longing for I know not what, I had;
 But when I see thee I am whole again ;
I cannot tell what makes me feel so sad,
 Oft must I shed my tears without a pain,
 Without a cloud it could forever rain;
Oh I am rent in twain, I can but wail,
 The other part of me I seek in vain,
Methinks thou hast it — tell me now thy tale."

LXVII.

" I have no tale, O lovely tears," she said,
 " But let me give instead this little ring,
Within doth sleep a gem, in golden bed,
 A little token of my heart I bring ;
 But let it nestle in its covering
Lest it be lost, and lose its setting too;
 When coming trials leave in thee a sting,
Perchance it may hint help to bear thee through.

LXVIII.

" Ah were I but an hour so fair as thou!
 But as I am I shall contented be ;
I look so gladly on thy shining brow,
 And yet a line of pain I there can see,
 An agony that struggles to get free.
Can suffering interlock with beauty so?
 At whom lookst thou?   That is young Paris, he
Who came from Troy to-day, as thou mayst know."

LXIX.

The crowd broke in with noisy reverence,
  Their prayers rapt by deep-lost looks to say
Before that form divine; without defense,
  Iphigenia lone was swept away
  On living surges crazy with delay;
Many a gallant Greek crushed in, one glance
  To get far dearer to him than the day,
And stood in worship sunk as if in trance.

LXX.

And Paris came and all his Trojan band,
  To gaze on her whom men agreed to call
The fairest woman of the Grecian land,
  With them a guest now in Mycenæ's hall,
  And Helen had a winsome word for all;
But when on Paris she had turned her look,
  Each was the other's victor and the thrall,
Each read the other's fate as in a book.

LXXI.

But hark! the bard begins a song in praise
  Of Argive Helen, Lacedemon's Queen;
Strong are the words whereof he builds his lays,
  And sweet the cadence falling in between,
  Dropping like skyey notes from choirs unseen:
" O thou, of all our hearts the very heart,
  Of our fair stock the branch forever green,
What Hellas is in all her best, thou art.

LXXII.

"For thee we give with joy this pearl of life,
  For thee our city and its law are naught,
For thee with tears our children and our wife
  We leave, and let them die at home distraught,
  While we shall haste to distant battle fraught
With danger unto thee and thy fair form;
  When once the bosom's guest is thy sweet
    thought,
Farewell our home of peace and welcome storm.

LXXIII.

"From our deep fealty to what is thine
  Doth trill, of all our life, the sweetest drop;
To us doth pour from thee a stream divine,
  Which fills our human lot unto the top
  With singing floods of joy that never stop
E'en in the tempest or the whirlwind's blast,
  Though we be dashed with all the ills that drop
From out the skies, and smite the world aghast.

LXXIV.

"For thine own honor lives heroic song,
  The tune of flutes, the touch of thin-shelled lyre;
In many-folded robes the Graces sweep along,
  Who the dear maidens in the dance inspire
  To be as thou art, fairest of the choir;
Youth hands to thee her overflow of wine
  Lit with the sparkle of Olympian fire;
Ere Hebe fills Jove's beaker, fills she thine.

3

LXXV.

" The mighty Gods for thee come down to earth,
  And in a burst of joy their forms reveal;
The Muses sing themselves to sudden birth
  In strains of thine, to lighten and to heal
  Our being's pain, which the born man must feel,
While he shall stain with tears his prison bars;
  The man must sorrow know as manhood's seal,
To take within his boundary the stars.

LXVI.

" The sword waits in its sheath on thy behalf,
  And always we shall have to draw it too;
Our life for thee we offer with a laugh,
  Demand it now, the gift is always due;
  If false to all, to thee we shall be true;
The price we pay for what of thine we get,
  Who beauty loves, must ever beauty rue,
This law the Gods on mortal men have set."

LXXVII.

So sang the bard, and from his heart he sang;
  He knew the Future, Present, and the Past;
He knew the joy of beauty and its pang,
  Love gave him bitter-sweet unto the last,
    Though the white years upon his head had
      massed;
Love made him young, but also gave him sorrow,
  While Poesy did wing him for the blast,
That where he fell to-day, he rose to-morrow.

LXXVIII.

But Helen glided softly out the throng,
A sudden pain she felt, a double pain;
She felt old burdens of that poet's song
  Return and press upon her life again ;
  And with them now a burden new did strain
Her heart-strings tense, already sorely weighed ;
  Soon Paris had her footsteps overta'en,
He knew his prize and in a whisper said:

LXXIX.

" In thy first look the Gods declared thee mine ;
  Not Hellas is thy worthy dwelling place,
Go with me to the East, where thou shalt shine
  The rising sun upon a starry race;
  Leave homely duty to the homely face;
Choose now a life of love with me to roam,
  Leave thy dull husband here, and his dull
    days,
Quit rocky Sparta — Troy shall be thy home."

LXXX.

But faintly Helen stemmed his strong command :
· " Oh can I leave behind what I have been —
The golden years that clasp me to my land,
  Leave husband and my babe to scorn and teen,
  Leave Hellas too, where I so fair am seen,
Where longer than the Gods themselves remain
  I shall upon my Grecian throne be queen,
For Zeus hath promised me his future reign.

LXXXI.

"But ah! no word of Zeus my step can stay,
    When close behind me steals my destiny;
Yes, Love, I feel I must with thee away,
    To-morrow on thy bosom I shall flee
    Through storms of all the Gods across the sea,
Though I presage some mighty overthrow
    To lurk in this rash deed I do for thee;
Fate rules my world, not Zeus — with thee I go."

LXXXII.

Then Paris left, for falling like a ray
    On night came Iphigenia, maiden free;
She met pale Helen gliding out the way,
    And marked upon her brow the mystery:
    "What aileth thee — art ill? Tell it to me;
Thy looks that were erewhile the sweetest grace
    To music wed, have lost their melody;
Methinks I see a battle in thy face."

LXXXIII.

Helen gave answer in a flooded strain:
    "Sweet maid, me to myself thou dost recall;
I had a sigh that tore my heart in twain,
    And I was cast away from home and all.
    But now I shall myself anew install,
And my whole life I shall through thee redeem;
    Music returns within, I hear its fall,
Zeus ruleth now, and Fate is not supreme.

LXXXIV

" To-morrow with the lark I shall be seen
  Hurrying home beneath the Spartan shield,
There still to be what I have ever been,
  Till it be time to rove the Elysian field
  With sceptred Menelaus, who will wield
A spirit sway with me for all my days;
  And I shall never die, shall never yield
To age, but stay the soul of Poet's lays."

LXXXV.

In secret Helen left with rising day,
  She kept her promise Paris not to see;
But ere she went a mile upon her way,
  A soft repentance she could feel to be
  Mellowing her heart into Love's piety;
And longing came, which deepened to a sigh:
  " Ah me, why did I treat him churlishly,
And did not even tell him once good-bye."

LXXXVI.

The road ran down along the loving sea,
  Whose billows, one by one, upon the shore
Would fall and plead at Helen's feet to be
  One moment, then would break forevermore
  Into the sand; far out was heard the roar
As ancient Ocean felt the power near,
  And splash of sea nymphs and of Tritons hoar,
Hurrying to the beach, now grown so dear.

LXXXVII.

Then from the foam did Aphrodite rise,
  And step with grace upon her pearly car
Made of sea-shell streaked with ruby skies,
  And tuned to music's lull without a jar;
    Nereids gathered round her near and far,
Who strook the brine from fervid coal-black hair,
    Whereon white hands would tremble like a star,
Twirling the tresses round their bosoms fair.

LXXXVIII.

And sea-boys, even one short glimpse to get
  Of perfect being hovered far in droves;
The mighty whale, the little finny set,
  And the strange dweller of lone island coves,
    The odd fantastic shape that shyly roves
In deep sea-vales — all felt the strong constraint;
    The heart of Ocean, full of many loves,
Swelled to a mountain high, then fell down faint

LXXXIX.

As Aphrodite stepped from out the wave,
  And entered in her fane upon the land;
The sea grew calm at her old task to lave
  The shoaly ledges with her pale blue hand,
    Calm at her ceaseless washing of the sand
That it be clean for the last day; then fled
    The sea-boys with the nymphs far from the
      strand,
Océanus droops down as he were dead.

XC.

The Goddess went within her temple fair,
  Whose slender amorous columns strove in vain
To kiss the sea which bore her gently there,
  In purple billows imaging the fane,
With every form of Love's strong joy and pain
That lay upon the temple's front up high,
  Carven so that they seemed to live again,
Or in their agony again to die.

XCI.

Those sculptured forms of old fond histories
  Must then have heard within the house a call
From that fair Queen, as she did lightly rise,
  And take her place upon the pedestal,
Where, as she stood, her garments she let fall,
Which, sea-stained, hid away her shape divine,
  Whose glow the cold hard marble can enthrall,
And make men drunk with beauty as with wine.

XCII.

And there in lofty state the Goddess stood,
  With her deep bosom bared unto the sight,
Whence rose the first sweet throb of motherhood,
  The thrill to sink away in Love's last rite
  And in a dream of it to vanish quite;
The robe dropped down the loins, when was re·
    vealed
  To mortal men the Goddess in her might,
Who deepest wounds hath made, and deepest
    healed.

XCIII.

To Aphrodite's temple Helen came,
    In her long journey of the lonely day,
Within her bosom burned the hidden flame,
    She longed the Goddess one short prayer to say,
    Perchance a little sacrifice to pay,
Some solace to receive from her sad thought
    Which dwelt upon a stranger's face alway,
Or left her for a moment more distraught.

XCIV.

She looked, and words broke deeply from her
        breast:
    " Goddess, I never knew thee until now;
Of all divinities thou art the best,
    Though oft before I paid to thee my vow,
    My life with thine thou never didst endow.
Of land and sea thou art the conqueress,
    Henceforth in all I shall be thine, be thou,
Be it to bring me joy or bring distress."

XCV.

Therewith from ruffled skies the thunder fell,
    Down through the temple roof red lightning
        broke,
And made from clouds a falling fiery well,
    Then mid the flames the Goddess sternly spoke
    In words which Helen smote like hammer stroke:
" My Paris whom I sent, why dost thou flee?
    This burning wrath of mine wilt thou provoke?
Yield me and follow forth thy destiny.

XCVI.

" With him to Troy thou must erelong depart,
This Hellas must thou leave and family;
Here Pallas wise and Juno chaste thy heart
Will share ; my sway must undivided be ;
A life of roses wilt thou lead with me ;
Why turn thine eye to look upon that ring?
Halved shall I not endure the sovereignty;
Beware my curse, beware the Paphian sting.

XCVII.

" A God can give or take away his meed,
Love can I give, but also I give hate ;
Detested shall I make thy life indeed,
As thou art now beloved by small and great ;
Nor this hard blow will yet my anger sate :
What makes thee Helen I shall take away,
What holds the world in thrall to thee like
Fate —
Thy beauty shall I shrivel in a day.

XCVIII.

" I bid thee break at once that hated ring,
Else I shall strike thy youthful body sore,
Leave thee a withered, wrinkled virtuous thing,
Whose lusty spring is torn from all the year,
Whose juices scarce will furnish one moist tear
Which thou wilt try in loneliness to shed —
' Tis broke ! Seek Spartan home without a fear,
I shall be there and everywhere ahead."

XCIX.

Then Helen fled out in the tempest dazed,
    To hollow Lacedemon in a dale;
The hill-tops whizzed, on peals of thunder raised,
    As if they would the skies above assail,
    And over all the Gods of Greece prevail;
The lightning chained with fire the peak to peak,
    Then leaped with molten links into the vale,
And clanked them round and round in vivid streak.

C.

Still Helen fled amid the storm forlorn,
    To her a saving power had been given;
Zeus shook his locks of lightning never shorn,
    Yet smote not that lone woman with his levin;
    In some deep protest raged the hills and heaven,
Still on she went through brakes and thickest holts,
    Around her everywhere the crags fell riven,
The woman charmed the God's own thunderbolts.

CI.

The house of Agamemnon woke that day,
    In misty morn to find fair Helen fled;
Still flocked the heroes greetings sweet to say,
    For each had risen early from his bed,
    To catch his dearest dream ere it had sped;
In vain, for she was gone, their hearts were shent:
    "It is some whim in beauty's fickle head:"
So guesses flew in deep bewilderment.

CII.

But in those bosoms wrath soon rose to prayer :
" Though thou be gone, Oh leave thy look
    behind;
It builds in us the world each day more fair,
    Till yestreen we saw Helen, we were blind ;
Rest thou the image painted in our mind
Of man and woman's love in fond caress;
    Thou art the very self of human kind,
Blent to a vision of all loveliness."

CIII.

They shouted for the bard, but he was sad,
    He would not sing his music-flooding ode
Which bubbles out Castalia's waters glad,
    But spake a word of melancholy bode :
" Gone! still her look of Fate she hath be-
    stowed;
It is in me, I see it in you all ;
    Whoever bears within his soul the goad
Of Helen's look, must soon obey her call."

CIV.

Now Paris, when he heard that she had gone,
    Bethought himself that he must also leave ;
Next day he bade farewell at early dawn,
    With tears at parting he did seem to grieve ;
Whereat the king began anew to weave
His plan, and called his daughter, but she had flown
    Unto her flowers, fresh buds to interleave
With thoughts about the life to be her own.

CV.

Paris gave out he would return to Troy,
　To tell the happy tale of what he saw,
The festival, the friendliness, the joy,
　　With sober things — the city, land and law;
　　But southward all his sails were seen to draw
By the Laconic coast into the sea;
　　Mycenæ gazed afar, presaged no flaw,
But turned to games and dance and minstrelsy.

CVI.

One man alone of all the Trojan band,
　While out at sea, sought Paris to dissuade,
And begged to steer his ship to his own land;
　　'T was Antenorides who loved a maid
　　At home, to whom his mind was ever staid;
"This Spartan tour," said he, "portends no good;
　　The Grecian woman is in us a blade
To pierce the Trojan heart and let its blood."

CVII.

The Trojans laughed at the prophetic word,
　And all applauded Paris and his scheme;
The madmen their true voice no longer heard,
　　They too found Helen's look deep in their dream,
　　And all was not which there to be did seem;
So shouted they: " Now is our happy mood,
　　We must again behold high beauty's gleam,
And pluck the reddest rose of womanhood."

CVIII.

So sailed they on, nor had they any care,
  They stirred long ripples in the silent seas,
And when ashore they saw the starry Bear
    By night with blazing eyes look through the
    trees,
    And heard wild voices coming down the breeze;
Still sailed they on, their deed could not be let,
  But wise, forethoughtful Antenorides
Was dragged along with them in fateful net.

CIX.

A horseman dashed into the Lions' Gate
    One day, with foam-flakes snowing from his
    steed,
And the pale rider scarcely could await
    The struggling word to break the woeful deed;
    "The Gods the loss of Hellas have decreed!
A Spartan home hath our fair Helen quit;
    Along my pathway mother Earth did bleed,
As if she in her very heart were hit.

CX.

" To Lacedemon came a Trojan man,
  And Menelaus gave a holiday,
The dearest maidens danced, the young men ran,
  And all the people turned their mind to play;
  Meanwhile the stranger planned his wicked way
To carry Helen off beneath the night;
  To Grecian gifts behold the Trojan pay,
And it shall be re-paid with all our might.

CXI.

" Still yonder ye may see the loving pair
  In lounging sail to dally on the wave,
Which Zephyrus caresses with his air,
    While soft Oceanus the keel doth lave,
    And flocks of doves fly in the sun to save
From view of men the hour of lovers' flight;
    Now will my country be an unsung grave,
And all its golden days will sink in night."

CXII.

Iphigenia too in sorrow spoke:
  " So thou art gone at last, it was my fear;
By some fell power my ring, I know, is broke,
    I gave it thee, stained with thy dropping tear,
    When thy full heart had drawn to me so near;
Ah never have I felt my life so crossed,
    No more than thou can I stay longer here,
With thee now lost am I, the world is lost.

CXIII.

" Nay, so I must not speak — it is not true !
  I shall not yield a thought unto despair;
Up, shrinking soul ! I still have work to do ;
    Lay hold of Time, O woman, bravely dare,
    Think not too much, for thought doth bring the
      care ;
Though thine be death, each blood-drop is a seed,
    By action thou old Fate shalt overbear,
The test of womanhood is now the deed."

CXIV.

But Agamemnon's words were open joy:
"Let the fair woman go, I fain would pray;
I shall restore her soon, and lofty Troy
  In mighty war I shall bring under sway,
  Whereto I long have sought some secret way;
I shall that Asian bound to my full power
  Now push far out into the rising day;
To Priam's son I yet shall give a dower."

CXV.

But while they talked, arose a distant dust
  Upon the road around a little hill;
That dusty cloud was whirled within a gust
  Of sudden wind into the town so shrill,
  That all the people leaped up in a thrill;
Then from the cloud was born a mounted group,
  And of the group one man each eye did fill,
Spurring ahead of all the sweaty troop.

CXVI.

Soon any child within the town could tell
  That Menelaus was the foremost man;
Quickly he rode into the citadel,
  While all the crowd his broken look did scan,
  And wonder what might be his anxious plan;
Then came Presentiment's dark underflow,
  While Rumor wildly raged about, and ran
Proclaiming tumult, war and overthrow.

CXVII.

All knew without a word why he was there;
　To him was pointed soon far out at sea
A speck that danced between the wave and air,
　A sparkling sail that lingered laughingly,
　And gave one parting glance in tiny glee,
Then twinkled out the blue to nothingness;
　Whereat his eyes, strained to their last degree,
Broke silent tears that told his deep distress.

CXVIII.

To that same spot had come the Grecian chiefs,
　Speechless they gazed at the retreating sail
Which left behind in them a world of griefs;
　It seemed as their own soul began to fail
　And flicker off upon the ship's sea trail;
But when at last from view the vessel sped,
　They stood not valiant Greeks in coats of mail,
But bronzéd corpses seemed, all standing dead.

CXIX.

As rustling leaves break in October dreams,
　When under trees we lie but half asleep,
And what we are awake blends into gleams
　Of life when it has broken Time's strong keep,
　And of the world beyond we get a peep;
So all the Greeks saw through their ghostly stare
　The future deed rise pictured from the deep,
And sprang at once their armor to prepare.

CXX.

War! war! they shout in wrath — a woeful word
  Which now through Hellas rings from bound to
    bound;
War! war! the rattling shield and spear are heard;
  There rises every kind of martial sound,
  War! war! the men in arms spring from the
    ground; .   .
What is then lost which all the people seek?
  War! war! they cannot live till it be found,
Helen must be restored if Greek be Greek.

Iphigenia at Aulis.

Sacrifice and Rescue.

ARGUMENT.

The Greeks are gathered at Aulis for the Trojan expedition, but are kept from sailing by the Winds. These form a chorus and sing at intervals through the Canto, which has two main portions, whereof the central figures are the father and the daughter, respectively.

I. The first wind-song introduces the reader to the scene at Aulis, where there is much contention among the Greeks. The characters of the old Greek chieftains are given, to whom a new one is added, Palamedes. The leader is chosen, the lot falls upon Agamemnon, to the great disappointment of Achilles. In his grief he communes with his Goddess-Mother, Thetis, who bids him stay with the Greeks and endure. Agamemnon in his new-born insolence seeks the chase, and slays a fawn, sacred to the Virgin-Goddess, Diana (Artemis); he wantonly violates virginity, which is the law of the Goddess and thereby incurs her wrath. The Winds now sing their song of vengeance, and detain the fleet; Calchas, the Soothsayer, interprets them, and declares that Agamemnon must sacrifice his daughter on the altar of the Goddess. The Leader refuses at first, and tries to sail out of the bay, but the Winds again rise and

(52)

sing a more furious song. Agamemnon now yields and is ready to sacrifice his child. (I—LXX.)

II. Meanwhile Iphigenia has started from Mycenæ to visit her father at Aulis. Her journey is described as she passes through many famous places, all of which have some character in history or legend. She arrives at Aulis in the midst of the furious song of the Winds, and finds her father in agony, and the whole armament in an uproar. Calchas, the Priest, sees her and tells her she must sacrifice herself for Greece and for the restoration of Helen. After a short struggle the maiden assents; Achilles sees her and changes from wrath to placability — an anticipation of his career at Troy. She is led to the temple of the Goddess, who saves her, but tells her that she must go far off to the barbarous world and serve as a priestess. All the Greeks recognize the greatness and beauty of the sacrifice, feeling that it hints something beyond their life. They set sail for Troy to rescue Helen, the erring woman, for whom the pure woman has given herself. Both Calchas, the priest and Palamedes, the moralist, recognize in the event something beyond their previous ken. The Winds sing their farewell song of harmony, and help the ships forward to Troy. (LXX. to the end.)

I.

List to the Winds and catch their moody lay !
Unrestful up and down the strait they blow,
They meet at Aulis, tumble up the bay,
   They twist the curls of Tritons to and fro,
   And all the fleet without an oar they row,
No sail can be unfurled, no rope be cast,
   Above the sea-war voices singing low
Are heard out of the bosom of the blast:

II.

"We blow to the East and West, to the South
   and North,
Over the water and land unseen we break,
Around, about, above, below, and back and forth,
   Forever change we are and change we make,
   Eternally the heavy ships we shake,
The drowsy men we rouse with our commotion,
   We move the deeps for the movement's sake,
And stir to life anew the ancient Ocean."

III.

Hear Boreas whistle in his chilly blast!
  Upon the sail he leaves his icy coat;
The Southwind breathes warm kisses on the mast,
  And sings its passion in a tender rote,
  The ice melts in the ripple to the note,
And Zephyrus doth come and lay his balm;
  The waves drop in a trance around the boat,
The sails are dead, and Aulis in a calm.

IV.

So sweep the winged Winds from rage to rest,
  And then from rest they rush to rage again,
The wave mounts upward to their wild behest,
  Or sleeps in peace beneath their soothing strain,
  With dreams of skies held fast in crystal plain,
But soon the blasts are loosed, and bring anew
  In wrathful energy their stress and pain,
For in this world must all receive its due.

V.

Now on this windy watery element,
  Where sea-lit Aulis lies along her strand,
The Greeks were kept, with double purpose rent,
  Whether to bring back Helen to her land,
  Or to send home all of their warrior band;
Oft had they spoken, yet could not agree,
  Contention rose, whatever might be planned,
And dashed them round as surges on the sea.

VI.

For every madding wind burst out released,
  When but a sail upreared would give a sign;
They ran from South and North and West and East
  As if sent on their way by power malign;
    But when the boats were moored, the sun
      would shine.
Then all the wise men wondered what it was
  That could the eager ships so long confine;
Some said a God and some that Man was cause.

VII.

The oldest lord was prudent, white-haired Nestor,
  Words sweeter flowed than honey from his
    tongue :
The holy priest was Calchas, son of Thestor,
  Who on the voice of God or Goddess hung,
    And knew what every bird in heaven sung;
Ulysses always deepest wisdom taught,
  Though it might not prevail at first among
His people, till they took the second thought.

VIII.

Ajax had come, the bulky man of brawn,
  Who bore a mighty fortress in his frame;
Small Menelaus too, whose wrong had drawn
  All Greece to seek revenge for Helen's shame ;
    Young Diomed, a doughty knight who came
From Argive land, whose fiery soul sought fight;
    Thersites, who had won a bitter name
Abusing leaders whether wrong or right.

IX.

But Agamemnon was the greatest king,
  Of all the chiefs he had most towns and land,
And most ambition to the war could bring ;
  Achilles had inborn the Hero's strand,
  Yet not with it the gift of self-command
Which trains to duty first the rebel soul ;
  Still he would be the leader of the band,
And all the rest, but not himself, control.

X.

Good Palamedes, too, was present there,
  The man who always sought to look at right ;
For beauty he had not a single care,
  Its tender thrill ruled not his sense of sight,
  Whereby his Grecian soul had left him quite.
They all were gathered now the chief to choose,
  The Argive herald shrill, Talthybius hight,
Bade silence so that each could tell his views.

XI.

King Agamemnon was the first to rise,
  A politician's wiles he knew to life,
Tears started as he looked up in the skies :
  " I think I shall go home to my own wife,
  And Helen leave with all this Trojan strife ;
Our stay at Troy will last for many suns,
  Far, far it lies, with all disaster rife,
Let us return to home and little ones.''

XII.

Broke Palamedes in, the rightful man:
" So many faithful wives why should we leave,
For that one faithless Argive wife who ran
   Away from husband, leaving him to grieve,
   And tell the time in tears without reprieve !
I say she hath not won a goodly fame;
   And shall we every household now bereave
For her who boldly threw away her name?

XIII.

" She went with Paris of her own free-will,
   Though she may blame the Goddess for the
      deed;
The stain upon her life remaineth still,
   Although she seek to hide it in a creed,
   And make divine whatever may mislead;
The woman who is led by Aphrodite's word,
   Or shall for guilt the Paphian power plead,
Must first herself by harlotry be stirred.

XIV.

" I shall not quit my home for such a jade,
   And leave to sigh and sorrow all mine own ;
Perish the oaths to Tyndarus we made !
   By breaking them is now the strong man shown,
   I shall do so, although I stand alone.
O Helen, for thine ills what deadly cure !
   Thou art not worth this solitary moan,
For thee distained we shall not give the pure."

XV.

Then forward sprang to speak young Diomed,
  Within his eyes the flint kept striking fire,
And sparkles threw with every word he said,
    Whereby that word did drop red-hot with ire,
    Yet had a music in it as a lyre
When burn harmonic ardors in the strings,
    Attuned to song aflame from warlike choir,
When it the blood-beat of the battle sings.

XVI.

" I say, let us at once sweep forth to Troy,
    For Helen give our lives in valor's glee;
Without her glance the world hath not one joy,
    The all-in-all of all our hearts is she ;
    What's wife and child, what's all that is to be,
If fairest Helen must a captive sigh?
    What then am I myself in verity,
If I the Greek cannot for Helen die? "

XVII.

Whereat the Greeks sent up a mighty shout,
    That rose an unseen mountain to the skies,
For each one heard the very word spoke out,
    Which in his heart had struggled hard to rise
    From that dim lake where speech unbodied lies;
Then stood Ulysses forth who knew the dutiful,
    Well he deserved to be entitled wise,
Though wisdom coined he not into the beautiful.

XVIII.

" A wife and babe I too at home have left,
Telemachus and true Penelope,
But of them both I am this day bereft,
　　Unless through Troy I bring them back to me,
　　And raze that hold of Greek captivity.
If I shall win them, Helen is the cost,
　　In her the one, all wives we must set free,
And in her loss, behold, we all are lost."

XIX.

No shout the Greeks gave wise Ulysses' speech,
　　For by them he was hardly understood;
His thoughts flew high in air beyond their reach,
　　And yet they somehow felt his words were good,
　　Except Thersites, of the scoffers' brood;
He turned grave wisdom into ridicule,
　　He railed at Helen and all womanhood,
And made the world just like himself — a fool.

XX.

" The game in this whole war is love," he said,
　　" The love of Trojan booty is the main;
Yet if the love of Helen tickles Diomed,
　　Why then should I and other Greeks be slain
　　For that one woman, vainest of the vain?
But we are told in one to see the all,
　　Such misty music is our wise man's strain;
So be it — in Helen see each woman's fall."

XXI.

Then Nestor rose and caught from him the word,
  And tore from it the lie in knavery wrapped;
The old man's voice the people gladly heard,
  He after wise Ulysses spoke, and capped
  Dim wisdom with some shining legend apt,
Or story taken from his far-off youth,
  Telling a wondrous tale that deeply lapped
In folds of rich romance the wise man's truth.

XXII.

High sounded the applause of Grecians, for
  He called them back from scorn to their own
    heart,
In sweetest tones of silvery orator,
  And many turns delicious of his art,
  Yet flashing wisdom out of every part.
The aged man sat down, a youth arose
  Whose single glance made all the people start
The battle cry, as if to charge their foes.

XXIII.

It was Achilles who in splendor came,
  The noblest form of all the Grecian host,
Each muscle was athirst for glorious fame
  In tear-worn war, whatever be the cost;
  But the great world in his own self was lost;
He knew who was the Hero, his name could call,
  A name on fleeting Time to be engrossed,
All men were there for him, not he for all.

XXIV.

Yet he had nobler strands within his breast,
 Which Cheiron, wisest teacher, raised to day;
Of music's concord was his soul possessed,
 He well could touch the lyric chords in play,
 And sing heroic deeds in lofty lay,
Till fired by his own strains he soared above
 And found a tuneful sphere, where every way
Led unto harmony and human love.

XXV.

But Cheiron's lesson was now well forgot,
 The Hero sought the army's chieftaincy,
He was for fairest Helen, yet was not,
 But for his own fair deed that was to be;
 He rose to speak, the entire company,
Rapt with his beauty, whispered each to other:
 " He is the man for all supremacy,
Godlike his shape, a Goddess is his mother.

XXVI.

" See but the motion of his hand — what joy!
 It pours within us more than Bacchic stream;
For him now could we take another Troy,
 More beautiful than Helen is that gleam,
 With our last breath we would his life redeem,
If he a captive were as she is now,
 Of gloried Hercules he comes the dream,
The ray divine is flashing from his brow."

XXVII.

Quick words of short contempt Achilles shot:
  "Let us no more in useless speech debate
Whether the woman shall be restored or not,
    But let us choose a chief at any rate,
    Then can I tell what is to be her fate
When I shall see our leader and his might,
    If he be merely first in wealth and state,
Or he who in the front rank best can fight."

XXVIII.

Ulysses seized the helm with lots, and prayed:
  "O Zeus, put the right man in the right place!
Let body's might be not our ruler made,
    Lest brawny arm take all for its own grace,
    And smite both rule and reason down apace!"
The Greeks with wise Ulysses prayed the prayer,
    When Agamemnon's lot leaped out the case
Of brilliant bronze into the eager air.

XXIX.

Achilles turned in silent wrath aside,
    Back to his sylvan home he thought to go,
In Aulis he would not one day abide,
    But leave ungrateful Grecians to their woe,
    Who were not able their best man to know;
He went alone along the ridged sand,
    His tears into the sea began to flow,
And swell the waves that strook in peace the
      strand.

XXX.

" Ah why was I not born of slaves a slave,
 Why was heroic heart put in my breast,
To be the scorn of every subtle knave,
 And from the struggle never to have rest?
 O mother Thetis, mount thy billows' crest,
And tell why thou, divine, hast brought me forth,
 Me Goddess-born, to be by time distressed,
By men to be cast out as nothing worth! "

XXXI.

Therewith he flung a tear into the brine,
 Which heaved to meet him like a mother's heart;
A thousand hands above the waves did shine,
 And reach out to him there as to impart
 Some touch of balm to soothe his fiery smart;
And all the sea became a sea of light,
 While from the ripples' break soft tones did
  start
And turn to speech just at the margent white.

XXXII.

" My son, I hear thee weeping at my shore,
 Would it were the last tear that thou wilt shed !
Thy honor yet will be neglected more,
 And contumely's dart will pierce thy head,
 Until thou liest cold among the dead.
Thy lot it is by men of little worth,
 To be misprized, till thy full time be sped;
This is the badge of thy heroic birth.

XXXIII.

" Gods, pity me, the mother of but one,
  Who is so great that he must early die;
Could I have borne a weak, ignoble son,
  Then mine had been a blest maternity.
  Yet wherefore am I mother but to cry?
And wherefore am I Goddess but to bear
  The sorrows of the world upon my sigh?
Oh stay, my son, it is thy mother's prayer."

XXXIV.

Therewith she rose above the mighty mere,
  Her son she kissed as the great waters drave,
And with her own she washed away his tear,
  Yet with her breath divine endurance gave
  Of the heroic pang, which stills the grave.
Up with her rose the Ocean many-tressed,
  Who fitted to her form his yielding wave,
And with her clasped the Hero's shaggy breast.

XXXV.

With one embrace she sank down in the main,
  The struggling waters rested from their coil,
Peace spread on billows blue afar her train,
  And busy ripples turned back to their toil;
  Achilles felt no more his bosom's broil,
When he had heard his loving mother's speech;
  He traced strange thoughts upon the sandy soil,
And picked up gorgeous shells along the beach.

XXXVI.

Proud Agamemnon sat within his tent,
  The Chieftains flocked the newest man to greet,
And many costly presents to him sent
  Of golden beakers, tripods, vestments meet
  For body, bed, for stool beneath his feet;
It was a wild exultant gathering
  That surged around to knee the royal seat,
And loud proclaimed a God to be the king.

XXXVII.

The Leader deigns to deem himself a God,
  Himself to be above all guilt he deems,
And of man's punishment to bear the rod,
  Dire Atè feeds his heart with all her dreams,
  And insolence from every action gleams,
E'en royal courtesy is throned on pride;
  No limit to his will to have he seems,
Not Zeus, but he Olympus doth bestride.

XXXVIII.

Full early in the morn he seeks the chase,
  To vent in wildest sport his wanton mood,
To hunt instead of men the sylvan race,
  When suddenly he comes to Dian's wood,
  Which on a hill not far from Aulis stood; —
A sacred spot, that was encircled round
  With walls and hedges, woven to exclude
All trespass from the hidden holy ground.

IXL.

Within the close were many pretty fawns,
　That cropped the leaves with kisses delicate,
Or played in coyish pleasantry on lawns,
　Without the dream of hairy horned mate,
　All to the purest Goddess dedicate.
It was a spot where none with stained thought
　Might enter in the pearl-embosomed gate;
The very air breathed innocence untaught.

XL.

But Agamemnon knew no sacred bound,
　Desire had now become his only law,
He leaped the wall and sprang upon the ground,
　The fairest fawn within the grove he saw,
　And there he smote her with goat-footed paw,
As if he were a satyr of the wood;
　Deep in her tender heart sunk down the claw,
And o'er her body white was written blood.

XLI.

The heart-struck fawn ran off unto the fane
　Spilling her virgin drops with helpless shriek;
Along the grass was trailed a purple stain,
　Which burned the greenest sod to a sere streak,
　And called on Mother Earth revenge to wreak.
To altar of the Goddess pure she fled,
　And gave one piteous look of prayer meek,
Then fell down at the feet of Dian, dead.

XLII.

At once the sky was dipped in blackest wrath,
   Amid the trees leaped red the ragged fire,
The heavens everywhere portended scath,
   As if they sought to make the world a pyre,
   And singe it to a crisp with lightnings dire;
The thunder chain, with dreadful links of sound,
   Clanked on the flaming air with wrong afire,
And dragged fleet molten fetters on the ground.

XLIII.

The timid fawns had scampered through the grove,
   With terror of the time their bodies shook,
Through hiding thicket one by one they strove,
   Or huddled in a mass within a nook,
   Around they dared not for a moment look;
It seemed as if the Goddess could not shield
   Her innocents along the forest brook,
But must to ruthless ravager them yield.

XLIV.

The Leader knew at once what he had done,
   He hurried pale from forest to the fleet,
The glance of Goddess there he thought to shun;
   He ordered all the chiefs betimes to meet,
   And bring aboard the armament complete:
"Aboard, Aboard, I shall no more delay,
   Seize hold the oar, hoist to the wind the sheet,
And strike the foamy wave to-day, to-day."

XLV.

The people deeply wondered, but obeyed;
    Like ants they swarmed along the shelving
       shore,
And not a moment in their task delayed;
    They dragged the ships down to the water hoar
    With shouts that capped the hill-tops in a roar ;
They cut in haste the hawser from the land,
    Then rose to smite the salt sea with the oar,
And thought to leave at once old Aulis' strand.

XLVI.

But when the air had heard one lusty stroke,
    It madly changed into a furious blast ;
Each sail did seem the wind-god to provoke,
    So that he stripped it from the reeling mast,
    And its white tatters in the sea did cast ;
The Furies of the air would hiss and howl,
    The Demons of the sea would scurry past,
And furrow its calm face with gloaming scowl.

XLVII.

The wrathful Winds again were heard to sing :
    " The man shall not escape, the guilty man ;
We come, we come, his wicked deed we bring,
    Our hands have been at work since Time began,
    We keep upright the world the Gods did plan,
The blast on sea and land is but our speed
    The hidden wrong from out the earth to ban,
We spirits are that blow to man his deed."

XLVIII.

Thus in a chorus dolorous they sang,
  With its vast bass of waters chimed the deep,
The skies attuned thereto with thunder rang,
  Long rocky hands would catch the keel, and
    keep
  It fast on shoals, or hurl it on the steep ;
Soon every ship put back into the bay ;
  Then would the Winds begin to fall asleep,
Or mid the masts low notes of guilt to play.

XLIX.

And every Grecian soul amazed did ask :
  " Why do the Gods to us opposed stand ?
For it is they who stop us from our task
  Fair Helen's wrong to quit with vengeful hand.
  Some unseen crime is lurking in the land,
Innocent blood its curses on us wreaks,
  The culprit must be found, his guilt be banned,
Although he be the first man of the Greeks."

L.

Then sounded through the multitude of masts
  The voice of strong Talthybius herald shrill ;
It sent a shudder like the shrieking blasts,
  And made the host that felt its keenness, chill
  With fearful bodements of a coming ill ;
To the assembly all the Grecians throng
  To hear what is the word divine, while still
The Winds, at parting, lisp a sigh of wrong.

LI.

Then Calchas, holy Priest, the first arose,
  The darkness was transparent to his view,
He kenned the will of Gods and of their foes,
  How the great Universe is ruled he knew,
  How man in it is governed saw he too,
Upon his heart the law was deeply writ,
  His eye shone sunlike looking on the True,
The world he saw not, but the God in it,

LII.

The brook he heard not but the Nymph therein,
  The roar of skies would speak to him of Jove ;
So he had heard the Winds beneath their din
    Announce the deed that wronged the Gods
      above,
  And had on Earth below slain human love;
He was the only man in all the fleet
  Who knew the voice in which the tempest strove,
And could its very words to men repeat.

LIII.

Beside the will of Gods to him was known
  The human soul, which he could clearly scan
When it in darkest depths was left alone
  With guilt, by Gods forsaken and by man,
  By all the lightnings pierced of its own ban ;
He looked in it and saw the deep disease,
  Straightway he sought to carry out the plan
Whereby to give to it the sweet release.

LIV.

Such was of holy priest the greatest gift :
  He sought the errant spirit to reclaim,
The burden from the breaking heart to lift,
  To bring atonement for all wicked blame,
  And new existence give and a new name ;
The guilty life he could far down unroll,
  And take the evil strain from out its frame,
And reconcile with Gods the cast-off soul.

LV.

He spake a speech that all the host could hear:
  " I tell what Zeus and mine own soul command,
Although my sharp rebuke shall smite the ear
  Of highest man in all the Grecian band:
  Ye sail away unto the Trojan Land
Wrong to avenge, and yet that very wrong
  At Aulis has been done with wanton hand ;
Now Helen's injuries to Greeks belong.

LVI.

" A fawn devote to virgin Artemis
  Is lying slain within her holy ground ;
The guilt of Paris, I proclaim, is his
  Who did the lustful deed, and made a wound
  On innocence which would all Troy astound ;
Think not the Gods will pass in us offense
  For which they shall the Trojan town confound ;
They punish in us too its insolence.

LVII.

" Our deities are high because the rods
  They bear for all who shall their law transgress;
Greek wrong is punished hardest by Greek Gods
  For deed of guilt give ye to them redress,
  Impartial is their wrath, their blessedness;
If they have judgment sent against proud Troy,
  By that same judgment now they send us stress
Of winds, whereof take heed lest they destroy.

LVIII.

" A contradiction is of Gods the hate,
  They will not long abide discordancy;
That man they leave unhelped to vengeful fate,
  Who seeketh not from guilt himself to free,
  And to bring back his life to harmony;
By sacrifice alone can he be rid
  Of wrongful deed, whose ruth he feels when he
Does to himself what he to others did.

LIX.

" O Leader brave, thou hast a daughter dear,
  A virgin pure as is the sky-born snow;
I cannot speak the word without a tear —
  The Goddess bids thy child to be laid low
  Upon her altar with the axe's blow;
The Winds will never cease from out the skies
  To pour upon the fleet their blasts of woe,
Till with the fawn thy bleeding daughter lies.

LX.

" If to the Gods for all thou wilt her lend,
  Thou wilt thyself of thine own wrong redeem,
For thou hast taken back thy deed to mend,
  And plucked it from the penalty supreme;
  True leadership will out thine action beam,
When for thy land thou yieldest dearest ties;
  And the new Helen will restored gleam
Through thine own daughter and her sacrifice."

LXI.

So spake the holy Priest, who truly saw
  In all its deeps what lies in human deed;
But Agamemnon spurned the sacred law
  And cursed the spotless man who said the creed:
  " Thou sordid Priest! I know thy calling's
    greed,
'Tis gold that buys thy word, somebody's gold,
  Who is mine enemy; the Gods take heed
Through thee on pelf and power to keep their
    hold.

LXII.

" Thy subtle priestly craft shall not rule me,
  Although thou make weak men in fear opine
Thy will to be the will of deity;
  My own sweet will is just as good as thine,
  And I believe it is quite as divine,
Nay more divine, for I have power.— The oar
  Now lift again, O Greeks, and smite the brine
For Troy, our injured Helen to restore."

LXIII.

The men went down into their ships once more,
   And stirred unwilling waves with busy blade,
But soon they heard approach a wild uproar
    From out a cloud wherein the flashes played
    So fast that every seaman was dismayed;
And suddenly the Winds smote in a throng
   The sails to ragged shrouds of gloomy shades,
Singing a new and more destructive song:

LXIV.

" We come, again we come, and thrice we come,
   With treble howl, around, above, below;
We burn with blast of fire, with cold benumb,
    The man, the man, the guilty man we know,
    For him we come to-day, for him we blow,
We are the Fates, we are the Furies too,
   We cleanse the earth with death as round we go,
What guilty man has done, to him we do."

LXV.

Forth rushed the Winds, at first with sudden kiss,
   As if a parting lover in his hurry;
But soon they changed into a dreadful hiss,
    And on the sea and shore would skip and
      skurry;
    A thousand airy serpents seemed to worry
The mortal man and strike with unseen fang;
   At last the Winds rose in one mighty flurry,
And, rushing on the ships, again they sang:

LXVI.

" Twice, twice, to-day have we with shrilly lay
To Aulis come and sung amid the fleet ;
Our first was gay and chimed a changeful play;
The second moved to a far deeper beat,
Ha ha! but you were saved by quick retreat ;
    The third time we are here with curse more
      savage,
Ha ha! 'tis vengeance whistling in the sheet!
    We come! we come! hear now our song of
      ravage!"

LXVII.

Then ship on ship was driven in the clamor,
    Men fell into the wave and rose no more,
Over the water flared a lurid glamour,
    As damned phantoms smote the sea and shore,
    And every sail from mast and halyard tore:
The ships could scarce escape the crackling flame
    Which out the belly of the Winds upbore,
By fleeing back to Aulis whence they came.

LXVIII.

The first to put about into the bay,
    Was Agamemnon, palsied at the sign
Which Gods had shown to him of their own way ;
    He sent at once for Calchas, man divine,
    To break the spell of that great might malign,
He fell down by the Priest with heavy groans,
    Yet his new life through tears began to shine,
As he with soothéd Winds did mingle moans :

LXIX.

" Zeus, Father, must I sacrifice my daughter !
Of womanhood the tender blooming rose !
The sweetest flower of my life I thought her;
　What then have I to live for if she goes?
　Help, Calchas, stroke thy hand along my
　　throes;
Thine eye bids me to think myself a King;
　I am a King — the Leader here bestows
His daughter and himself an offering."

LXX.

Meantime Mycenæ gay its song had lost,
　The dance had ceased and merry festival;
In place of joy its hearts were sorrow-tossed,
　The mother, wife, the little children all
　Oft gathered lonely on the city wall
To gaze for messenger or ship afar;
　No voice was heard but woman's cry or call,
For every man had gone to tearful war.

LXXI.

No word from Aulis came, they cannot hear
　What is the reason of so long delay;
Iphigenia thinks without a fear
　A visit to her noble sire to pay,
　Ere he to distant Troy be gone away ;
Out of the Lions' Gate she drove her team
　Of mules that shook the sweaty yoke all day,
Up hill and down, and by the rippling stream.

LXXII.

Her chariot first ran through the stony glen,
   Where once the Gods and Titans fought their
      fight
In ages hoar, then left it unto men;
   She saw rocks hurled with superhuman might,
   And dark chaotic powers put to flight
Long long ago, when first this sunny world
   Of Grecian Gods dawned gleaming on the sight,
And gloomy deities to Tartarus whirled.

LXXIII.

And then she went through silent piney dells,
   Where she would hardly dare her breath to hear,
Lest she disturb the spirit that indwells
   The oak, the bubbling spring, the lonely weir,
   Or skims high woodlands like a star in fear;
The Hamadryad's lightest lisp she heard,
   As it would vanish on a gossamer,
And oft she caught and kept its dying word.

LXXIV.

The women of each village hugged her path,
   With babe at breast and children at the dress,
A kindly look and speech for all she hath,
   Their husbands were at Aulis in the stress,
   And they could see ahead long wretchedness;
True wives, they sent by her some word or token,
   To those they loved, whom they in faithfulness
Must give for that one wife whose faith was
      broken.

LXXV.

Past Ephyre's high breast she quickly rides,
　Whose city lies between Poseidon's knees,
While Aphrodite's foam laves both its sides,
　And Acrocorinthus stops the stirring breeze,
　Until it swoons away amid the trees
To soft Idalian kisses round a shrine;
　Through that lax luscious air the maiden flees,
And touches not her lip to Corinth's wine.

LXXVI.

She rests not till she comes unto the bound
　Which sends her high up to a mountain land,
Where ancient fable sported with the sound
　Of sweetest minstrelsy, or chanson grand,
　Hymning the mighty gests of Hero's hand.
One path she shuns where Theseus of yore
　With stolen Helen fled along the strand,
The Trojan deed presaging long before.

LXXVII.

From heights she passed into a fruitful dale,
　Which fluttered everywhere with silvery leaves
Of Olives, changing sunlight to a pale
　Moonlight that with the treetops interweaves;
　Like sobbing heart afar the orchard heaves;
Women are there culling the fruit alone,
　Yet each looks up at passing team, and leaves
Her task awhile to think of some one gone.

LXXVIII.

To plain of Ceres then the maiden drove,
  Where the broad land springs into yellow corn,
At hidden tender touch of Goddess' love,
    As if out of the earth the golden morn
    With a new sun were of a sudden born ;
O'er all was felt the sacred mystery
    Of man, who also springs from night forlorn
To day, till he again in night shall lie.

LXXIX.

Through many a grove of plaintain and of myrtle,
  Over Kephissus' gentle element,
To voice of nightingale and Attic turtle,
    Mid strains of seas and skies and mountains
      blent,
    Royally into Athena's town she went;
From Pallas' hill she looked far on the sea,
    Unto its very bound her glance she sent,
And saw the empire there which was to be.

LXXX.

The Muses sang around her their own rule,
  As she did loiter on their sacred hill,
Where was intoned the note of every school
    Which hath through Time's deep bosom sent
      its thrill
    Of harmony — mind's cunning, hand's skill ;
Then looked she to the East and saw the proud
    High threat the Greek horizon darkly fill,
But soon the Attic sun smote through the cloud.

LXXXI.

Over the radiant hills to Marathon
  She darts as if she held Apollo's ways,
There on a plain she saw that Attic sun
  From skies descend transfigured in a blaze,
  Which all the earth illumined with its rays ;
A little village glowed within the sunset crest,
  As drew to end the greatest day of days,
And turned down Grecian hills into the West.

LXXXII.

Another note was sung in Marathon
  Mid golden cornfields leaping from their grave ;
She stopped along the sea when day was done,
  She heard the never-ending waters rave,
  And thought, Will Asia ever cross this wave
To Greece, as now to Troy we Grecians go ?
  Such deeds bring forth their like, however
    brave ;
O who shall break this endless chain of woe !

LXXXIII.

She came to Rhamnus, town of ancient fane,
  The home of Nemesis, the Goddess hoar
Whose blow requites on man his action's bane !
  No rest she found, she quit the temple door,
  And hurried past unto the lonely shore,
Where of that Titaness she might be free,
  Whose furious word is vengeance evermore ;
Sweet peace she found beside the yielding sea.

LXXXIV.

All day her chariot wound about the bank,
    Whose sunny path the whitest pebbles pave,
To smiling stillness the wide waters sank
    Before the presence of the maiden brave,
    Or rose in ripples mild her feet to lave,
When she would walk along the beachéd sea;
    Oft tresses of the Nymphs would float the wave,
Then melt into the blue transparency.

LXXXV.

As Aulis rises slowly into view,
    She hears the angry bustle of the blast,
She sees the waves swell up with trouble new;
    And drive within her sight a slivered mast,
    Which breakers smite, till it on land be cast;
Then reeling ships she spies, which seamen row,
    In secret nooks they huddle all aghast,
As if to shun a second hidden blow.

LXXXVI.

Iphigenia rode in peaceful mood
    Deeper and deeper to the storm's fierce heart,
Where lone within his tent her father stood,
    Whose tears at sight of her began to start,
    And ashen quiverings of pain to dart
Through chorded limbs, tense in the bitter strain;
    Then would he seek suppression of the smart,
Grow calm apace, till tears fell down again.

LXXXVII.

" What is it that so pains thee, father dear?
    What winds are those I heard not long ago?
I see that thou art struggling with a tear;
    Those blasts still threaten as they whirl and
        blow
Far out upon the sea, where now they go;
Their biting edge I touched upon my way,
    Still I in thee can feel their afterthroe;
What is thy sorrow?   Let me its pang allay."

LXXXVIII.

While yet she spake, the captains one by one
    Dropped in to speak a word unto the chief;
They viewed the maid who soon all hearts had won,
    Yet not by love like Helen, but by grief;
    Fair words they spake of deep regard but brief,
They felt the awe, and in her look could see
    All time before them pass, like falling leaf
Which drops to earth, and leaves the heavens free.

LXXXIX.

Achilles, too, had sought the Leader's tent,
    To bid a grim good-bye to chieftains there;
He looked upon the maiden's face, he went
    Not forth, but on him settled unaware
    A distant view of something more than fair,
Than Honor worthier, higher than Glory,
    He wandered with it far up in the air,
While it to him alone told all its story.

XC.

He said unto himself: "I now must change,
  Old Cheiron never could have taught me this,
He never could have shown the vision strange
  Now shown by simple maid, a little miss,
  Whose face doth look the very God's in bliss ;
To me her glance is more than Helen's glance,
  Henceforth its guidance I shall not dismiss,
Its spell may yet my deepest hours entrance."

XCI.

Then Calchas came, he scarce could hide his moan,
  He hinted that he had a word to say apart,
And when he spake unto the maid alone, ·
  The parting of his lips cleft to his heart :
  "I must speak forth the word with all its smart :
That ill winds cease to blow, and fair ones rise
  To bear the Grecian fleet to Troy, thou art
To be to Artemis the sacrifice.

XCII.

" That Helen may be saved, thou art to die,
  The pure must give itself for the distained,
It is the world's last law, which to defy
  Is breach for which the man will be arraigned
  Before that court where justice is not feigned ;
Shun wrong of shirking what is on thee laid ;
  Innocence lost by guilt, is then regained,
When the pure soul its offering is made.

XCIII.

"In Troy's own wickedness we Greeks are strong ;
  The Goddess now demands our highest meed;
Then only may we right the Trojan wrong,
  When we ourselves the way to right may lead;
  We can avenge another's wrongful deed,
Not till that deed out of our heart is burned ;
  Never can we take Troy till we are freed
Of Troy's own guilt, and to ourselves returned.

XCIV.

" From Zeus supreme comes down one great be-
    hest
  That good men owe themselves unto the bad ;
Else were they hardly good, and never blest
  Through the high suffering that pure and glad
  Maketh all hearts by making them so sad ;
Above fair Helen will thy beauty rise,
  Thy land in thee its rescue will have had,
And the whole world in thee its sacrifice."

XCV.

So spake the holy Priest, a noble man,
  Who wrought not for himself, for all he
    wrought;
The Future in the Now he well could scan,
  That which must be forever, was his thought,
  And that was what he to his people taught;
Yet truest Greek he was, most true of all,
  What Hellas was to time itself he sought,
Not to the East he looked, not to Troy's fall,

XCVI.

But in the West he saw futurity
Grow out the deed of heavy suffering,
Saw a new world rise out the farthest sea,
    And a new Hellas in it upward spring,
    And to mankind afresh its blessing bring;
Far-off dim visions and blest auguries,
    Snatches of song he heard the poets sing,
Hymning in ages late the sacrifice.

XCVII.

His was no cruel speech but tender grace,
    With every word his own great heart was rent,
And if he could he would have ta'en her place,
    For her endured the bitter punishment ;
    Into her sorrow was his soul so blent
That she could nought but his sweet presence bless,
    As his strong thought into her breast he sent
Armed with his pity and tender-heartedness.

XCVIII.

Thus sighed she answer to the holy Priest :
    " Oh must I die, who love my life, so young?
And must I now be slaughtered like a beast
    At the blest shrine to which I oft have clung,
    When with the pain of life I have been stung?
Have mercy on me, Goddess, hope is spilt —
    The howling winds through all the shores have
        sung
The strain of vengeance for some hidden guilt.

XCIX.

" But ah! the more men need. to be set free;
    If they were guiltless, they no help would need;
What is life good for, but to give it thee?
    To keep it for myself is but a greed,
    To yield it up makes of it fruitful seed;
Here take it, I give the last of earthly joys,
    This bloom tear from my cheek, and let me
        bleed,
Guide me to the altar's ax — it is my choice."

C.

Achilles came and looked, a changed man,
    He hears what he before had never heard;
He saw his life anew and made its plan,
    To bitter sacrifice he too is stirred
    By that sole thrill of tender maiden's word;
His mien superb becomes her humble thrall,
    Now his heroic sword he will engird,
To fight not for his glory, but for all.

CI.

" Ah me!   I know I am short-lived by fate,
    But I prefer to die as thou wilt die;
If I should stay at home I might live late,
    And pass my days without a single sigh;
    But I shall equal thee in destiny,
And give myself in bond to sharpest woe,
    For thee I shall my very wrath deny,
Be placable to friend, and e'en to foe."

CII.

So thought Achilles then, when he had seen
  In wonderment of love that spirit staid ;
But on the Trojan plain in quarrel keen
  Hereafter will forget the vow he made,
  And turn to wrath that will not soon be laid,
Unmindful of his country, friends, and cause,
  For vanished is the image of the maid ;
Dark lines through his bright fame a Fury draws.

CIII.

Yet memory of her afresh will live
  When he doth weep o'er dear Patroclus slain :
He, rueful, will his Grecian foe forgive,
  Now softened by the mighty mass of pain ;
  Yet to forgetfulness will fall again
And her sweet image blot in Trojan strife ;
  Then will compassion cleanse at last that stain,
And give to Priam old both son and life.

CIV.

Rumor went buzzing through the gathered
    Greeks,
  It told the sacrifice of high degree,
Whose blood would end delay of many weeks,
  And bring fair winds upon a tranquil sea,
  Yet fetching too the fierce fatality.
Their hearts were torn, it was a time of wail,
  Low words they moaned of crushed anxiety,
That day all wished the fleet might never sail.

CV.

Still the Euboic hills detained the sun,
  Who threw upon their peaks his last of light
For that one day, and then his course was done;
  In silence flew the silken wings of night,
  To brush out of the skies the cloudlets bright,
And tinted films hung high on heaven's way;
  Then sank into the mist the mountain height,
And twilight poured its flood on Aulis' bay.

CVI.

Meantime they bore the maiden to the shrine,
  Which lay upon a knoll within a wood;
There Calchas led her through a weeping line
  Of massive men who round her pathway stood,
  To see the highest worth of womanhood;
The hearts of all burst out in tearful rue,
  As they beheld in her what was the good,
And made the vow to her they would be true.

CVII.

The fair white fane of marbled Artemis
  A smile into the twilight seemed to throw;
From its fond pillars flowed a silent kiss
  Which showered love around the deed of woe,
  As there in flight of stone she grasped her bow
To save a fleeing fawn from savage chase;
  She touched the arrow in a sacred glow,
The very marble lit up in her face.

CVIII.

Within the door the maiden disappears,
 A cloud descends and fills the holy space,
And for a moment sheds its gentle tears,
 Till every leaf and grass-blade in the place
 Hath on it one pure drop of sorrow's grace,
And bends to let it fall upon the ground,
 Which swallows it at once and shows no trace,
Though leaf and grass, freed from the weight,
 rebound.

CIX.

But soon with ragged rent is pierced the cloud,
 And through it looks the silver-shining moon,
Which softly floods the melancholy crowd,
 And to a music sweet doth them attune,
 While they quite sink away into its swoon;
It drives far off the night with the dark cloud,
 And out the air into her lunar noon
The Goddess stepped at once and spake aloud:

CX.

" Thy time is full, thee have I come to save,
 As promised in Mycenæ from my shrine;
Men say I in revenge thy life must have,
 Because thy father slew with heart malign
 The guiltless fawn he knew I loved as mine;
But no! the Goddess must not vengeance pay,
 Not death for death can be the law divine,
Though he slay mine, his shall I never slay.

CXI.

" The Gods must not revengeful be to man,
  Else they will not escape his penalty;
The Gods must also learn, and learn they can,
  To give up hate, and turn to charity,
Whereby alone we Gods are whole and free.
The Greeks shall deem thee dead, with grief be
      racked,
  But sacrifice they shall hereafter see,
And find the richer blessing for thine act.

CXII.

" But to myself I shall now rescue thee,
  I, the mild Goddess dare not take thy blood;
Thee shall I bear away to Barbary,
  There in a land remote to do the good,
Anew the offering for a multitude
Vaster than all on earth to be now found;
  The world, all time thy deed will yet include,
Far wilt thou pass beyond the Grecian bound.

CXIII.

" This hour auspicious gales begin to blow,
  Helen, the erring one, is to return,
The armament shall crush the Trojan foe
    Through deed of thine to-day, which men will
        burn
    To imitate, and from a maiden learn
To offer life for land and family;
  With Helen home, thou too wilt homeward turn,
And Greece. once saved, is saved again by thee."

CXIV.

The moon has fled with night, and timid rays
Of rosy dawn into the heavens rise;
While in the woods a godlike presence prays,
  Soft hymns of triumph float up to the skies,
  Bearing aloft a world of harmonies;
The Greeks rush to the fane to hear the word,
  The ax unbloody on the altar lies,
The maid is gone, and naught of her is heard.

CXV.

Astonied they all stand at plan divine;
  But see, there is another wonder new:
The fawn that dead was lying at the shrine,
  Rose up to sudden life before their view,
  And to its perfect strength at once it grew;
Unharmed through all the gazing crowd it flees,
  No stains upon the grass it now doth strew,
And soon from sight is lost amid the trees.

CXVI.

A wave of silent sorrow sways the host,
  No heart so dumb but feels the common pain ;
They would have spared her death at any cost,
  But somehow felt it was her greatest gain
  And theirs, to die for them without a stain ;
A universal tear doth make them one —
  One people now, and ready to be slain ;
By that sole maiden's deed it has been done.

CXVII.

" This law of deity each man must find,
  Sorrow alone can purify the heart,
And make it deeply one with its own kind,
  Whereby in all it feels its own keen smart ;
Charity then comes and draws the dart,
Compassion cures, yet is the child of pain;
  The Gods give first a loss, in loving part,
Whereby to give in turn a greater gain."

CXVIII.

Thus Calchas first that solemn silence broke,
  As in deep thought he out the wood did wend,
And to the people round him further spoke:
  " I thought the maiden's death to be the end
  To which the Goddess did her power bend ;
But I the priest must learn a lesson late
  Through this dear maid, that Gods must not
    offend
By vengeance, but be themselves compassionate."

CXIX.

Then Palamedes spoke, the rightful man :
  " I too have learned the lesson of this day,
And a new glimpse have had into the plan
  Of Zeus who over all doth bear the sway;
  In pride of right I spurned the castaway,
I thought myself so good, her not t'endure ;
  I change, I go to Troy for Helen, and pray,
For the distained may there I die the pure."

CXX.

All Grecian hearts are beating to one throb,
  They are one wave of vast humanity,
With undertone of sigh or secret sob,
  That breaks up from that sympathetic sea;
  Silent is glory and moral vanity,
Assemblies are not needed, there is heard
  An inner voice of last authority,
Which every man obeys without a word.

CXXI.

They go down to the beach in quietude,
  The waters rest in calm transparency
Reflecting hill and cloud in peaceful mood;
  They go into a thousand ships which lie
  Upon the bay beneath the tranquil sky,
They touch the pictured deep with muffled oar,
  The silent tear to Hellas says good-bye,
And drops at thought of seeing it no more.

CXXII.

Yet with a heavier sorrow they are fraught,
  A deeper loss than Helen's fills the host,
Each soul within the fleet has this one thought,
  What's Helen saved with Iphigenia lost?
  What recompense is greater than the cost?
Unless there be some other restoration
  Beyond fair Helen's, beauty the uttermost
Will never save itself nor save the nation.

CXXIII.

Again the feeling winds begin to blow,
    Not now with vengeful whistle of a squall,
But piping a delicious music low
    That drives the fleet to its soft tuneful fall,
    Whose long melodious beats the oars enthrall,
Yet underneath a note of sweet distress
    Sings in the Winds, and tunes the souls of all
To tender grief akin to blessedness:

CXXIV.

" Oh let us sing our song, our farewell song!
    We too, the blasts, are conquered by the maid;
However long we blow, however strong,
    We in that higher harmony are laid
    To which the Gods serene the world have made ;
Whatever be the time, the clime, the creed,
    Be it the king or slave, the due is paid,
For pain, for gain, we blow to man his deed."

CXXV.

Thus sang the Winds, it was of songs their last
    Nought more they had to sing, their voice was
        lost ;
They breathed their gentle breath on sail and
        mast,
    The ships no longer were by tempest tossed,
    By lightning burned, or frozen fast in frost ;
Hark now the ripple of the sunny sea,
    As up and down it rocks the parting host!
Look, there is Troy! Helen, thou must be free.

Iphigenia at Tauris.

Service and Release.

ARGUMENT.

Iphigenia is now brought to Tauris, the land of the Barbarians, in care of the Hours (Horæ), who here constitute a chorus, and who, according to Homer, open and shut Olympus. Their song, soothing, forewarning, runs through the whole Canto, which has two chief portions: first, the mission of the priestess to the Taurians, along with the love of Thoas the King; secondly, her dealings with her crazed brother Orestes, whose coming and cure are narrated, and then with King Thoas, who is also to be cured.

I. A description of the wild Taurian land is given. Its people make human sacrifices to their deity, they disregard all training of body and mind, in contrast with the Greeks. Though longing to return to her own country, Iphigenia at once goes to work to transform land, people and King into all that she is and all that Hellas is. She imparts cultivation of the soil and mastery of nature; she teaches the old Greek poetry and mythology; but above all, she inspires the rude Barbarians with humanity. Moreover she trains other priestesses like herself, who bring light to the remotest corners of that dark world.

From the beginning, Thoas, the King of the Barbarians, has been in love with the beautiful priestess, who has to shun his advances and thwart his purposes as they interfere with her priestly vocation, and will, besides, prevent her return to Greece, which she feels to be an integral part of her great mission. But Thoas, in his wrath at the refusal, gives signs of relapsing into his old habits of savagery, and she seems about to lose the chief fruit of her work, when she goes to the shrine of Artemis and prays. But the Hours whisper an answer to her prayer, that the Gods are doing their part. (*I.—LXV.*)

II. Meanwhile Orestes, the brother of Iphigenia, has arrived from Greece, with his friend Pylades, in obedience to an oracle of Apollo, who commanded him to bring back his sister. Thus Orestes, it was declared, would obtain relief from the pursuit of the Furies for having slain his mother. Brother and sister come together in the temple at Tauris, they converse, she learns of the fall of Troy, of the death of her father slain by her mother, of the death of her mother slain by her brother, who now falls down in a fit of madness before her. Pylades tells her the ambiguous oracle and Iphigenia interprets it, and discovers herself. Orestes hears the healing word, and rises from his fit; he is cured of revenge, and, hence, of the pursuit of the Furies.

But scarce has he announced his spirit's restoration, when Thoas, mad with love and revenge, breaks into her presence and threatens all three Greeks with death according to the Taurian custom. But him too the priestess heals; he repents; he sends her to Greece, even goes himself to help restore her to her land. So all the Barbarians show themselves ready to help rescue Hellas from its enemies. But Hellas has also an internal enemy of whom it must now free itself, and whose ominous strain is heard in the distance. (*LXVI.* to the end.)

I.

Hark! a new note! though all the Winds be laid
Which back to man his guilty action sing!
O, list, a deeper thrill! Where is the maid
  Who came to Aulis, daughter of the King,
  And gave herself for all an offering?
Another song! A sweeter softer strain!
  That note of love the Heavens seem to bring!
Out of the whispering North it falls again:

II.

" Tread softly, softly, in our silent round,
  Speed swiftly, swiftly, and the burden bear;
Our winged feet must never touch the ground,
  When we have come, we are no longer there,
  What is to be, is evermore our care;
Softly we tread, as light as breath of flowers,
  Swiftly we speed, unseen upon the air —
The softly-treading, swiftly-stepping Hours."

(101)

II.

Far in the north imbedded lies a sea,
  Around whose chilly marge the tempests rave,
And lash its forests dark of savagery ;
    Upon the dreary shore a lonely cave
    Leans down its ragged mouth to touch the
      wave,
That sends into the deep recess a moan
  On endless billows, which the lintel lave,
Or swell to kiss the dome of drooping stone.

III.

One narrow heaving path of watery flow
  From Hellas leads unto that far-off place,
Whereby a Grecian ship would sometimes go,
    And break the silence of the vasty space,
    But soon would flee in fear of savage race ;
Or if the vessel ran into the grot,
  All perished there unseen and left no trace ;
This Tauris was, to Greek a fearful spot.

IV.

Here was the fane by oldest Titans built,
  With pillars dropped from gemméd ceilings
    down ;
Upon its altar human blood was spilt
  Unto an idol there in stony gown,
  An ugly idol with a horrid frown,
That loved to see the victim in his gore,
  Or watch him in the surges helpless drown ;
The Taurian Goddess she who held this shore.

V.

" Tread softly, softly, in our silent round,
  Bend slowly, slowly, and the burden bear;
Here is the place — now set it on the ground,
  Behold the form of sleeping maiden fair
  Who in her journey long hath been our care.
Hark to the call of Time — we must not stay,
  Breathe on her eyelids but a breath of air;
She stirs! she wakes! we go, but she must stay."

VI.

Within the grot asleep the maiden lay,
  Iphigenia, there divinely borne;
She woke and went to seek the radiant day,
  But saw dim fog-light on a world forlorn;
  The heart dropped in her breast to see that morn,
No columns wrought upheld in joy her soul,
  She only saw huge rocks by water worn,
No sunny temple, but a dark, dank hole.

VII.

Such was the change from her fair Grecian home:
  No trailing vineyard waved within her look,
With leaves and vines that over hillsides roam,
  With Bacchus garlanded along the brook,
  While maids from trees the golden fruitage shook,
Or did in merry song ripe clusters cull;
  No God or Goddess in each sacred nook,
In sun-born shape revealed the Beautiful.

VIII.

The Olive, pyramid of fruit and green,
 Rose not, the very tree of Pallas wise ;
The sunshine came, but not with that soft sheen
 Which glows within the liquid Doric skies,
 And falls on sea and land a Paradise;
No smiling sunlike rays of yellow corn
 Shot up to greet the glad festivities,
And wrapped the earth in endless golden morn.

IX.

The howl was heard of savage roaming beast
 Above the endless sough of forest drear;
Each preyed on each, from largest to the least,
 The lion in his hunt would straggle near,
 His bloody trail would print the stones with fear ;
The falcon in the skies would claw the dove,
 The cruel pard below would tear the deer,
The eagle clove the hare, then soared above.

X.

Wild were the beasts, and wilder yet the men :
 Of whom a sudden rout sprang out the wood,
And hurried to the fane through tangled fen;
 A shaggy fell hung round the body nude,
 They howled in savage dance and gesture rude,
While in their midst a prisoner was bound ;
 Expecting death, he oft in terror stood,
Or oft was fiercely dragged along the ground.

XI.

Yet once from his tormentors he did leap,
  And fled away as fleet as any deer,
And sprang into the sea far down a steep;
  The maiden looked with sympathetic fear,
  To her at once the wretched man grew dear;
She hoped he might escape but he was caught,
  Whereat within her eye welled up the tear,
As she on him and on herself too, thought.

XII.

Him struggling to that very fane they bore,
  A sacrifice to Goddess there to pay,
They saw what they had never seen before,
  A maiden put herself within their way;
  She bade them not the guiltless captive slay,
But offered them herself instead of him;
  Blood ceased to flow on Taurian shrine that
      day,
And reverence did soften bosoms grim.

XIII.

Thoas was there, of all that region king;
  He kept his people back by his strong word,
When he beheld the maiden offering;
  By her one look his heart was strangely stirred,
  Then by her gentle hand he was deterred;
Awe seized him, as in her the Gods above
  He saw, and then a softer note he heard:
The awe divine began to whisper love.

XIV.

" Oh! where am I " the lonely maiden cried,
  " What will become of me if here I stay !
I thought within the fane I once had died,
  Then twice am I to die — die every day —
  What shapes fleet yonder on the air this way?
O speak me help and heart, ye Spirit Powers ! "
  To her in soft response arose a lay;
Thus sang the swiftly-stepping, soothing Hours:

XV.

" The maid who once was by the Goddess spared,
  She must now others save in that same need,
Again must do what she at Aulis dared,
  An offering for her own kind to bleed;
  It is the consecration of her deed,
Her sacrifice she will henceforth repeat,
  Until it is become her life and creed,
And every day her death she dares to meet.

XVI.

" She is to tame to peace these bosoms wild,
  And make them lose their mad delight in blood ;
It is her task to put her spirit mild
  Into the soul of men however rude,
  And make it bear her image of the good ;
When she the fierce barbarian hath won,
  Vengeance no more shall be his daily food
He shall forever do as she hath done."

XVII.

So sang the Hours, still longed she for her land,
  The Hellas far away, which had her slain
In its own thought, yet by divine command,
  When she at Aulis entered Dian's fane;
But now the long, long years she must remain
Within this distant savage wilderness,
  Busy until her time be come again;
Yet could she not the bitter sigh suppress:

XVIII.

" How heavy o'er me hang these leaden skies!
  O where is sunshine, where my own fair clime
And its fair works that everywhere uprise
  In splendor on the land and sea sublime!
The song and dance of youths in golden prime,
Labors of men, the sowing of the seed,
  The forms of Gods far looking down on Time,
The heroes great and the heroic deed!

XIX.

" It is a gloomy land, a savage brood,
  Where I must pass my youthful holiday;
The people know nought of the fair or good,
  But from all human feeling turn away,
  They kill themselves, and me perchance will
    slay.
Yet I have now to change them by my life;
  Yes, home is here, I feel, and I must stay,
And bring a world of peace out of the strife.

XX.

"The time has come, another Greece to make
  In new-born hope spring from this weary wild ;
I shall both for its own and for my sake
  Transform it daily to the image mild
  Which hath on men from Hellas ever smiled ;
I think the Olive may be hither brought,
  Though of the sunny skies it be the child,
But surely works of hand may here be wrought.

XXI.

" The labors of the oxen at the plow
  Are first to tame to peace the savage earth ;
In brotherhood the horse, and sheep, and cow
  Shall gather round the tranquil human hearth,
  And even brutes receive their higher worth ;
This horrent waste I see rise up before
  All others hitherto in a new birth :
'Twill be what Hellas is, it will be more."

XXII.

So flashed afar in dreams her shadowy thought :
  More than what Hellas hath she will impart
Unto that savage folk ; it will be taught
  A deeper Beauty and a holier Art,
  Which is the inner flow of human heart ;
The people will to nobler regions rise,
  Her deed, her life become their highest part —
She will endow them with her sacrifice.

XXIII.

The bound of Barbary she will transcend,
    And make all Greek beyond the Grecian pale;
The gentile hate in her will have an end
    When her new spirit shall in love prevail,
    And free the prisoned world from its own jail;
Old Hellas too, will share her blessing great,
    The distant threat she sweeps from hill and
        dale —
For the Hellenic land she breaks down Fate.

XXIV.

And there alone she stayed for twenty years
    With that sole purpose in her sincere breast;
She moved through troubled seas of hopes and
        fears,
    Still on she went in faith with all her zest,
    And never failed to think and do the best;
The people came to see her from afar,
    They went away with her high soul possessed,
And to her looking up as to their star.

XXV.

The noisome grot she turned to temple fair,
    With columns white that stood along the seas
And saw their limpid beauty imaged there,
    With wavy architrave and flowing freize,
    And sculptured shapes of liquid deities;
The ugly idol rose no more to view,
    The Taurian shrine no bloody death decrees,
The Goddess is herself transformed too.

XXVI.

With her are all the Gods of Greece transformed
Into fresh founts of mild beatitude,
By a new inner sun their looks are warmed,
  Not now the horrid Taurian monster rude,
  Whose stony frown was with cold death
    bedewed,
But sweet Greek Artemis is throned above,
  The Goddess who refused the maiden's blood,
And looked beyond Olympus, seat of Jove.

XXVII.

Demeter, too, sought in that land a home,
  Where she did sow broad-cast her foodful seed,
Which springs on heights or low in valleys' loam,
  Wherewith she might the teeming millions feed,
  And no one in her bounty suffer need;
The cattle grazed on every hill in peace,
  On endless plains of pasture roamed the steed,
And mother earth gave forth her full increase.

XXVIII.

And all the land was filled with gardens sweet,
  Which Pallas made her favored dwelling place,
Where stood fair boys of bronze that moved
    their feet,
  And steeds of stone that ran the swiftest race,
  And tripods moving to and fro with grace;
Within each brazen bosom breathed sweet life,
  The fiercest struggle calmed in marble face,
That told the Greek and the Barbarian strife.

XXIX.

The maiden taught the labors of the loom,
  In which her own strange life she deftly wove,
Her youth's deep dream, and then her sudden
      doom;
  Her web could tell how the great heroes strove,
  Reveal the deed of wrath, the deed of love,
Her Taurian life she did therein unfold,
  How it flowed on within the plan of Jove:
In gold and purple threads the tale was told.

XXX.

She tells anew the Grecian histories,
  The mighty gests of great Bellerophon,
Yet coupled with the saddest destinies;
  The highest deed doth hold the deepest groan,
  And greatness is but suffering alone;
That Hero vanquished monsters of the East,
  And made the fair Hellenic world his own,
Then senseless roamed the field as any beast.

XXXI.

She tells the fairest story of the sea,
  Of ship that bore the princely Argonaut;
She lapped the tale in folds of poesy
  More rich than all the gold the vessel brought,
  Yet with her own deep store of wisdom fraught;
Barbaric minds now build that ship of Greece,
  Which newer Colchian treasures further sought,
And bore to their own land the Golden Fleece.

XXXII.

But of the many wondrous tales she told,
  The chief was legend of stout Hercules,
The mighty darling of romances old,
  Who had to labor through all lands and seas,
  Until the earth of his fierce foes he frees;
He drained the bog, the mountain way he rent,
  He turned the rivers, felled the forest trees,
By him this earth was made man's instrument.

XXXIII.

The wildest beasts, the wildest men he tamed,
  When Greece her wilderness began to shed,
And the first law for human living framed;
  But when he over every land had sped,
  And bravely freed it of its monsters dread,
He must descend to Hades, free it too
  Of its damned dog which guards the gloomy
      dead ;
Both worlds, above, below, he must pass through.

XXXIV.

To the Barbarians the myth she sings,
  Which they take up and sing in their own tongue
Through all the distant realms of icy kings,
  Beside the northern seas, and up among
  The frosty blasts, whence Boreas is flung
Upon the south, where scarce the sun will shine ;
  Deep unknown rivers float the strains there
      sung,
And bards chant from the Danube to the Rhine.

XXXV.

The Gotans of the furthest Dacian plain
Catch up the echo of Hellenic lay,
And warp and weave it in their Gothic strain,
That floats beneath the Hyperborean day,
And wraps itself in misty folds of gray,
Far, far beyond the sunny Ionian skies,
Where now Europa sleeps her time away,
And where in might hereafter she will rise.

XXXVI.

In magic spell of strange barbaric measures
Are hymned those antique fables never trite;
And all the storied world of Grecian treasures
Is richly there inlaid with fancies bright,
That flash and soar in new poetic flight,
Though still they keep their first Hellenic soul;
The ancient germ doth now unfold to light,
And its deep hidden wealth in time unroll.

XXXVII.

A weird spirit entered in the word,
Which danced as if possessed and sparkled
round;
Then by some harmony most deeply stirred,
It wooed another like itself in sound,
Until the happy pair were linked and bound;
So word would chase another word to kiss,
In many strains of love they locked and wound,
And gave to man a foretaste of his bliss.

8

XXXVIII.

Through all that wilderness sang Helen's story,
  In sweet melodic concords of the rhyme;
It builded up afresh an olden glory,
    Though now transplanted from its Grecian
    clime,
    And moving to another tune and time;
The very sounds of it were wont to wed,
  As winged with Eros, they uprose sublime,
And glowed in raptured flight with passion red.

XXXIX.

It melted to its thrill the wildest heart,
    Which felt the honeyed spell of that great
    love,
And felt the pain, which was its other part,
    Sent down on guilty pair from Gods above;
    The human deed inside the will of Jove,
With all the strains of noble minstrelsy,
  In one vast strand of destiny was wove;
That guilt, to be o'ercome, had first to be.

XL.

Far on the air resounds that song of songs,
  Through all the spacious realms of Barbary,
It flames the hearts of bards, who rise in throngs,
  To sing that lay of deep fatality,
  And then the still more deep recovery;
It is the eternal song which they must sing,
  They hymn in it their own true history,
What Time has brought and will forever bring.

XLI.

The lay of Helen far resounded then,
  And still resounds afresh through all those
    lands ;
It weaves its magic chain in souls of men,
  And holds them tranced in its fine golden bands
  Which seem to grow to be life's very strands :
The oldest song and yet the latest too,
  It bears the human and divine commands,
True in that elder world and in this new.

XLII.

Ah me, could I but catch one straying shred
  Of that high strain and fix it in my line,
As it comes floating down, to music wed,
  I, the barbaric singer, might now shine
  And call my sisters all the Muses nine.
But one is born too late, aye, or too soon ;
  'Tis all the same, without the light divine,
To watch at night or go to bed at noon.

XLIII.

But hark ! again that sound upon the air !
  It fleets like straying note of hidden bird !
A voice now falls around the maiden there !
  And now it speaks a strong prophetic word,
  Whereby she in her very soul is stirred.
From Past to Future turn the secret Powers,
  And in their voices Time himself is heard ;
Hear them foretell, the swiftly-stepping Hours :

XLIV.

"Thou, maiden, art to teach a nobler lay —
It is the lay of Helen's restoration
Through thine own sacrifice, upon that day
When thou didst offer life for the salvation
Of the lost woman and the lost nation;
By that high deed was made the future path
Whereon man travels to his godlike station,
And with him bears the world from its own wrath.

XLV.

"And deeper, warmer still shall flow the stream,
The tuneful stream of song in pulses great,
Which all the wilds to clear away shall seem,
And cleanse the savage heart of all its hate;
It is the song of maiden dedicate
In barbarous Tauris now as once in Greece;
It hymns her life supreme, there consecrate
That world as well as Hellas to release.

XLVI.

"It tells how each is to regard the other,
Deeper than difference is unity,
The man is to behold in man his brother,
And bind him to himself in kindred tie;
Thine is the golden word of charity,
Which stops the hate of men, the war of nations,
Which melts to one the human family,
And interlinks the future generations."

XLVII.

Thus they foretold, the daughters of high Jove,
  The swiftly-stepping Hours the world foretold
Soon to be built anew for all by love,
  Which would make warm the human heart now
    cold
  And overmake to youth the ages old.
The maiden heard the voice, it was her lay —
  She was herself the story which was told,
And she began her task that very day.

XLVIII.

Many a Grecian man she did there save
  From wretched wreck along the rugged coast,
When he had strayed too far upon the wave ;
  She heard of sack of Troy by Argive host,
  And wanderings of Greeks by tempest tossed ;
But she was deeply filled with other thought:
  Greek or Barbarian, if he were lost,
In one great deed of love to save she sought.

XLIX.

And then she would transform him to her life,
  She lights herself into the hearts of all,
Whereby she puts an end to mortal strife
  'Tween East and West where stands the Trojan
    wall,
  Which she will take, not by the city's fall,
She will no lands lay waste, no towns destroy,
  She gives both sides her image magical,
With it she takes, and thereby saves old Troy.

L.

Band after band of priestesses she trained,
  Whom to the deepest wilderness she sent;
Of hardship, toil, and death they never plained,
  They gave up home and welcomed banishment;
  For savage man and child their lives were spent,
To whom they bore the lamp of their great school;
  Into the frozen, fiery zone they went,
And burst upon the shore of farthest Thule.

LI.

They stood beside the broad Atlantic seas,
  Whose waters measureless seemed their last
      bound;
But soon to land of far Hesperides,
  They crossed the wave, where a new world
      was found,
  And they at once began to break the ground;
Through wilder, vaster forests on they went,
  O'er mighty rivers, till they made their round,
And spanned with bridge of light a continent.

LII.

These women were the greatest conquerors,
  Theirs too, the lasting victory has been,
Though it was never gained in cruel wars,
  The bloody cutting sword was not their mean,
  They used a brighter weapon and more keen,
Their mind it was by which this deed was done,
  Girding the earth in zones of mental sheen,
To make the wide world one and keep it one.

LIII.

How all that people loved her, called her blest!
  Her as a Goddess they would fain adore,
She ever called up in them what was best;
  King Thoas was the man who loved her more
Than any other on the Taurian shore;
A noble man, and a yet nobler king,
  Of ruler's virtues he possessed the store,
He sought like her to be an offering.

LIV.

The days roll on, the mighty years roll on,
  Devotion in him suffers a slow change,
No longer awe of her religión
  He feels, but to a transformation strange
He falls, which doth his life and hers derange;
The king now loves her with a lover's love,
  Into his bride he will the priestess change,
And from her maiden destiny will move.

LV.

Still she doth long for her far native land,
  To her Greek folk she knows she must return,
They are to be made free by her own hand
  From Trojan strifes, from Fates and Furies
    stern;
  The Greek in thought has slain her, and must
    yearn
Her once again in his own world to see;
  All Hellas has through her anew to learn
To be transformed as well as Barbary.

LVI.

Helen they have restored with mighty arm;
   A deeper restoration must be won,
Which Iphigenia brings without a harm ;
   She teaches them to do what she has done,
   Her double sacrifice they must not shun,
The vengeful must to helpful heart be turned,
   Then is Greek wrong to her for aye undone,
Her image is into their bosoms burned.

LVII.

In royal suit she day by day is pressed,
   Which she must meet by craft, a trial new
That bears the deepest discord in her breast ;
   Her heart by double duty cut in two
   She feels; to Truth the first she must be true,
Yet to her Mission true; if she deceive
   The King, it will her very life undo,
Yet her last destiny she cannot leave.

LVIII.

Suspicion darkly broods in high-born breast,
   The King begins to change his confidence ;
The burden of his heart gives him no rest,
   In every act of hers he sees offense,
   Even her good he notes as insolence ;
The savage, long suppressed, begins to burn,
   To cruel thoughts are changed his new intents,
To ancient Taurian times he will return.

LIX.

One day he sends his trusty messenger,
  Demanding answer to be brought forthright;
Again she seeks her pretext to defer,
  And turns her step to hasten out of sight
  Into the fane, when suddenly in might
The King appears, and wrathful to her speaks;
  As if he had a battle there to fight,
His eyes flash vengeance which the savage wreaks:

LX.

" Thy subtle Grecian craft will do no good,
  Thy answer on the morrow I must have;
For thee I stopped the flow of human blood,
  I from the gory altar did thee save
  When savages did fiercely round thee rave,
I made thee greatest power in my state,
  Thy power through the world I to thee gave:
But now I feel my love turn into hate.

LXI.

" The wild man's heart once more begins to rise,
  My deadly foe shall be again the Greek,
Vengeance comes back, within I hear its cries
  To rash its claws into thy visage meek;
  Thy labors to undo is what I seek,
Ingratitude I shall re-pay to thee,
  A maddened savage I revenge shall wreak —
This altar's victim now thou art to be."

LXII.

In rage he turns away, she doth appeal
  Once more unto the Goddess at her shrine:
" High Virgin, thou who didst in light reveal
    Thyself to me, and take me to be thine,
    Didst make thy very ministry be mine,
And promise me return to my dear land,
    Me, fragile bearer of thy plan divine,
O help me execute thy high command.

LXIII.

" O Goddess, let me not from thee be taken,
    The Fate of Trojan love now threatens me;
Must I from thee, Protectress, turn forsaken,
    To Aphrodite given o'er, to be
    In foreign land held in captivity?
Another war of Troy, yet far more dread,
    More stained with human blood I can foresee;
If I return not home, I am but dead.

LXIV.

" Thou Goddess chaste, to thine own love enthrall
    This noble man's still savage love, I pray,
Which seeks me for itself and not for all,
    Immortal thou beam out my mortal clay,
    That he through passion rise to thy clear day.
Be not barbaric Tauris doomed like Troy,
    Let not good Thoas cast his gain away,
And by enslaving me himself destroy."

LXV.

Hark to the whisper on the sunny air!
  It is again the Hours, the watchful, true,
Who breathe an answer to the maiden's prayer;
  " We shut and ope Olympus to the view;
We guard the cloudy gate the Gods pass through
When they come down to stay the faithful heart;
  Release will come, but thou must also do —
The Gods for thee are doing now their part."

LXVI.

While still she prayed, far out at sea a ship
  Was seen to struggle through the plunging
    wave;
Deep in the watery chasm it would dip,
  Then from the top of highest surge it drave
Till scarce its keel the madding floods could
    lave;
Again would sink and almost disappear,
  Then rise and rear in air from its wet grave,
While ever to the land it drew anear.

LXVII.

In steady strife with that wild element
  The oarsmen long had beat the sullen brine;
But now they many feverish glances sent
  To see what on the shore might give a sign;
They saw around them rise a walled line
Of sea-smit rock on which they read their doubt;
  Oft had they heard it was a land malign,
Still pulled they on, and dared with bosoms stout.

LXVIII.

From far-off Hellas they had hither come;
  They took to ship at Aulis, in the bay
Where many years agone a troubled hum
    Of men would o'er the waters aimless stray;
    But this ship northward cut its lonely way,
And passed Olympus lofty on the left,
    Where happy Gods dwell in eternal day,
And of the song and feast are never reft.

LXIX.

The slender ship threads narrow Hellespont,
  Darts through the jaws of fierce Symplegades,
Where only Jove's swift-flying dove is wont
    To pass, when borne on strong Olympian
      breeze;
    The ship broke into solitary seas
Which surged upon a distant unknown world;
    The bounded Euxine felt a strange release,
And with new life its ancient billows whirled.

LXX.

Two Grecian Youths were sitting on the deck;
  The one did seem to toss the ship in thought,
His face was graven with a fearful wreck,
    And showed deep netted storms-lines inter-
      wrought
    Into his life, which the rough days had brought;
The other let no glance turn from his mate,
    Affection overflowed his eyes, yet fraught
With wearied sorrow, watching long and late.

LXXI.

One was Orestes, slayer of his mother,
  Whom Furies had at home pursued to rend;
Fond sympathetic Pylades the other,
  He was the Grecian Hero, but as friend,
  Whose heart, not guilt or glory, did him send
Along with Agamemnon's wretched son,
  Until the frenzied mind mightly haply mend,
Or of this life the frantic trip be done.

LXXII.

Upon them lay a stern divine command,
  The Delphic God bade them the sister find,
And said she was detained in barbarous land
  At Tauris, where she kept her fervent mind
  To be restored to her own Grecian kind.
Apollo's sister Artemis they thought,
  To the wise God's deep meaning they were blind,
But clearest truth from error dark is wrought.

LXXIII.

Far had they sailed, and still must onward sail;
  Where Tauris was, they did not fully know,
They kept by faith along an unseen trail,
  Until the chilly blast began to blow;
  The sailors murmured, would no further go,
Worn by the seas, they ran into the shore;
  Although they should be eaten by the foe,
They lay down in the sand and quit the oar.

LXXIV.

Not far away a spring flowed down a hill,
  And peacefully did mingle with the wave;
It was a soft, yet merry buoyant rill,
  Which had a speech as it the stones would lave,
  And e'en of music it would sing a stave,
Then fade away into a bubbling noise;
  A word in fond low tone it often gave,
Then in the flow of waters lost its voice.

LXXV.

It was of loving Nymphs the favored spot,
  Who the worn stranger with a balm receive,
And soon refresh him in their shady grot,
  Or in the brook their bosoms to him heave,
  Or hum a strain to which his soul will cleave;
To follow up the hill they lure their guest,
  And with soft notes his footsteps interweave,
Sing snatches sweet when he sits down to rest.

LXXVI.

Both youths went up the brook to fields of grain,
  A garden vast they saw from the high hill,
The island hamlets flecked the sun-gilt plain,
  In seas of verdure herds were lying still,
  Or cropped lush grass, or stood within the rill;
The yellow grain waved into red-barred skies,
  Which sent around the world a tender trill,
As playing music of that Paradise.

LXXVII.

Not far away a noble temple stood,
  Which seemed the shining center whence did ray
All of those glories of sweet plenitude;
  They had to follow but the nearest way
  To come to where the sunny structure lay;
They entered it, the landscape's very heart,
  To the divinity therein to pray,
If it might be appeased to take their part.

LXXVIII.

And there within uprose a sacred shrine,
  By it the priestess stood with kindly glance;
She seemed to shed on all a hope divine,
  Which would the shyest shrinking heart per-
    chance
  Embolden to its prayer to advance.
But hark! she speaks true tones of honeyed Greek,
  Bids them be now at home, and gently grants
Their dumb request to tell what here they seek.

LXXIX.

They answer liquid notes, how sweet the sound!
  She heard again her dear Hellenic speech;
Her home, her youthful days, her faith she found
  When she in words heart-born her thoughts
    could reach,
  And could without barbaric discord teach
What with her eye, what with her soul she saw,
  And in the purest mother tongue beseech
The Gods, without a stammer or a flaw.

LXXX.

But a still deeper music struck a note,
    Which tuned the priestess' soul unto one
        thought:
" I cannot tell what makes my fancies float
    Far back to childish things which once I sought.
    What hidden spirit hath upon me wrought,
That I to this sad youth should feel so near?
    Some destiny hath him unto me brought;
Him I must ask about my father dear."

LXXXI.

She spake to him of Agamemnon then,
    Foreboding by her soul's own magic spell
That this young man knew of the King of men,
    And could her father's latest story tell;
    That same deep feeling did the youth compel,
That he her heart within his own caressed;
    But now her speech dropped on him like a knell,
Yet he replied thereto with soul suppressed:

LXXXII.

" The mighty leader felled the town of Troy,
    Then safely home into Mycenæ came,
And there his spouse conspired him to destroy;
    She said that he at Aulis was to blame
    That her own daughter bled like beastly game;
The wife her husband smote with vengeance
        grim,
    She would blot out in blood his very name:
As he her daughter slew, so slew she him.

LXXXIII.

" Years sped by but vengeance was not stayed;
 The son Orestes up to manhood grew,
On him the Gods their heavy duty laid,
 The slayer of his father next he slew,
 The murderess who was his mother too ;
Justice it was and the divine command,
 She did receive but what was her own due,
So Clytemnestra fell by her son's hand."

LXXXIV.

The priestess softened doomful words in tears :
 " Oh curse of Hellas, horror to the light !
A land of sighs which deepen with the years,
 Where is revenge's rule and man's despite,
 The kindly human eye is put out quite ;
Nor yet is broke that fatal chain of wrongs ;
 Revenge begets revenge — somewhere in night
The Furies dog Orestes now in throngs."

LXXXV.

Therewith the youth in speech convulsive shook :
 " See where they come and fling their snaky hair
At me ; with burning demon eyes they look
 Into my heart and what lies hidden there ;
 They slime the temple's threshold— now they
  stare —
Keep off, keep off, I see the clotted stain ;
 I did the deed and would again it dare,
I slew her in revenge for father slain."

LXXXVI.

His eyes turned inward while his body broke,
  He coiled low down into a speechless fit;
Sad Pylades in tender heart throbs spoke:
  " Again by his own reptile he is bit,
    Not soon, I fear, the spell will intermit;
He is Orestes, same of whom he told,
  He tries to hide, but ne'er hath hidden it,
His strong attempt doth but his guilt unfold.

LXXXVII.

" He often lapsed before in such a swoon,
  When I went with him everywhere as friend;
His cure were now for me the greatest boon,
  Still I shall with him go unto the end,
    From beast and man and from himself defend;
When the wild fit comes on, he raves and shrieks
  At the Erinnyes, whose serpents send
The maddening hiss which vengeance wreaks.

LXXXVIII.

" Much have we roamed the world in search of
      cure,
  All Hellas we have seen, no help we found;
We sought afar the high-hilled fountains pure
  Of healing Nymphs who babble from the
      ground,
    And Aesculapius who mends each wound;
All, all in vain; till now my hope was fair,
  While he came hither every hour was sound,
To him returns disease, to me despair."

LXXXIX.

The priestess quick in thought to him replied:
" Revenge he takes, revenge him then pursues ;
That house of Tantalus which hath defied
   The Gods, is his; that house would ever choose
   Its own curse first, its blessing would refuse,
In its own ruin than all foes more strong;
   No heir of it forgives his bloody dues,
And stops the stream of wrong begetting wrong.

XC.

" From father to the son descends the curse,
   The son gives it anew unto his child,
And with each gory deed it groweth worse,
   Till human hearts which Help should render
      mild,
   Barbaric passion fills with rancor wild.
The time is come to make the great release
   From vengence which hath all our land defiled ;
Orestes' cure is too the cure for Greece."

XCI.

Good Pylades in wonder stared, then said:
" The Grecian Gods for us are powerless,
When our worn footsteps had to Delphi led,
   Apollo his own weakness did confess;
   The God declared we must ourselves address
To one who lived in barbarous land, not him ;
   But what he meant by that, we could not guess ;
We asked again, he spake new riddles dim :

XCII.

" 'Bring back from Taurian shore *thy* sister
　　dear,
Whose image there in starry sheen doth rise
Along the Northern seas, where thou must steer ;
　　It is a sacred image, from the skies
　　It fell on Tauris with blest auguries;
That land was then a dark and savage land,
　　She let my sunshine in, now bright it lies,
And merciful will give a helping hand.

XCIII.

" ' Bring back *my* sister thence, who did not
　　take
　　At Aulis once the dark avenging blood;
Who ancient cruel rites of Goddess brake,
　　When guiltless maiden at her altar stood,
　　And sacrifice became the doing good;
Then will Orestes be forever healed,
　　But he by Furies must be still pursued,
Until to Hellas whole she be revealed.' "

XCIV.

The priestess saw at once the God's intent,
　　His double word to her was one, and clear;
She spake in tones of mild admonishment:
　　" Blame not the God before thou rightly hear,
　　Thy mortal speech is not the speech of Seer
Or God, which thou wilt never understand
　　Until thou see it double, far and near,
See future and the past knit in one strand.

XCV.

"I tell thee now what wise Apollo meant,
When he from inmost shrine his riddles read:
I am Orestes' sister, he is sent
  To bring me back to those who think me dead;
My blood was not upon the altar shed,
By the God's sister I was saved and brought
  To Tauris here, amid Barbarians dread,
Whom fair Humanity we both have taught.

XCVI.

" The sisters twain of whom the God hath spoken
Are we — the mortal and immortal dwell
Together in a life of deeds unbroken ;
  I am the priestess who in word can spell
  The thought divine the Goddess doth indwell ;
' Tis I who shall return, the image bear
  Of her who venges not, but will dispel
The hate which Furies nurse into despair."

XCVII.

Not yet was lost the lisp of her last word,
  Orestes woke, and to his feet arose,
That final healing speech of hers he heard
  In trance, which was the end of all his woes,
  To a sweet rest were soothed convulsive throes :
The new man from his healthy eyes now beams,
  As he up to the holy priestess goes,
And to her speaks fulfillment of her dreams:

XCVIII.

" Thou art my long-dead sister, now I know
    What I at first but felt dim in my heart;
With me thy lot it is to Greece to go,
    And there to thine own land thyself impart,
    Draw from its raging breast the venomed dart,
For it is truly mad, as I was mad,
    With hot revenge ; it must be what thou art,
Be cured like me of having what I had.

XCIX.

" I saw the Furies flee to their dark cave,
    I heard the clashing door behind them close,
Within the earth's stone bowels let them rave,
    And smite her granite bosom with their blows,
    For I am free forever of their woes;
Thy word, thy healing word, hath done it all,
    Hath put to sudden flight my fiercest foes,
And me from frenzy back to life doth call.

C.

" Not stony idol set in fane, I see,
    Can be the image of the Goddess true,
She hath another higher ministry,
    Thou art her holy image, brought to view
    In deeds of life, and every day anew ;
Thou dost her worthy form divine reveal
    In freshest bloom of living human hue,
And poor mankind in helpfulness dost heal.

CI.

" Apollo's sister I shall with me take,
And with the Goddess mine own sister too, .
Both for my sake and for my people's sake ;
As she hath done, are they henceforth to do,
Yea, she must all men with her deed endue ;
It is her deed that us of evil rids,
The Fates shall fly from her as Furies flew,
She brings to end the curse of Tantalids."

CII.

While thus they talk, another raving man
With violence into their presence breaks ;
A fit of madness shrieks from visage wan,
Grimaces fierce and gestures wild he makes,
Each limb, each muscle in his body shakes ;
Thoas it is, already mad with love ;
But when he sees the Greeks, anew he quakes
For jealousy, and frights the holy grove :

CIII.

" Woman, Fury, thou art my greatest curse !
Thou owest me thy life and influence,
Thy purpose newly planted I did nurse,
I saved thee from the hand of insolence,
I calmed to hope thy fleeing, frightened sense,
I gave thee love, I gave this kingly heart :
Now I am scorned by thee, reap but offence,
And my kind breast is pierced by thy fell dart.

CIV.

" Traitress, ingrate, incapable of love,
  False to thy doctrine, in thyself untrue,
My good thou dost requite with wrong above
  What demons dare; I know what I shall do,
  For I see other knavish Greeks here too —
Thy lovers, come to carry thee away;
  On ancient Taurian altar, all of you,
I shall as pious debt long due, now slay."

CV.

The priestess caught his eye and touched his arm,
  Which, soon unnerved, writhed slowly to his
      side,
As if it held itself from doing harm;
  His savage lips did quiver, but not chide,
  Her gentleness o'erwhelmed him in its tide:
" O Thoas, friend — what hast thou done, al-
      most?
  A storm thy years of good doth override,
And oh, methought I saw thee in it lost.

CVI.

" Thy dark reproach I merit not, O King;
  Far more than all thee have I loved and thine,
For thee I have been here an offering,
  My days I have all given at thy shrine,
  My youthful days which will no more be mine.
If not my body, to thee my soul I give,
  That is my dearest boon, my part divine,
By which I hope thou mayst forever live.

CVII.

" To my own hapless land I am now called,
  To Hellas which me once did immolate,
Whereby to-day it is to guilt enthralled;
    Barbarian thou hast rescued me from fate,
    And thou must rescue too the Grecian State;
If I to thee have taught my highest worth,
    Thou wilt anew the priestess dedicate,
Restoring her to country of her birth.

CVIII.

" If thou dost truly love and honor me,
  Thou wilt surrender me to blessedness;
If what I am, in truth possesses thee,
    Thou wilt pass by thy right, thy sharp distress,
    And thine own sacrifice alone wilt press;
By keeping me thou hast me not indeed,
    By sending me, thou hast me none the less,
This is to thee my last, my highest meed.

CIX.

" If I may not my native land restore,
  The spirit cries, I shall myself not save;
If thou detain me on the Taurian shore,
    Thy liberator me thou wilt enslave,
    And thou no liberty thyself wilt have;
It is my time to go, my time just now,
    As long as the Greek brother is a slave,
I am not free myself — not free art thou.

CX.

" No family is mine, another law
   Hath claimed me with its strong behest ;
No babe with rosy lips will ever draw
   Its life out of the fountain of my breast,
   Or lisp to me of names the tenderest ;
Of Nature's loss I have to bear the pain,
   And rise upon it into duty blest ;
Another motherhood is there again."

CXI.

Barbarian Thoas drops the ruthful tear,
   He has received her final blessing too,
In giving up what is to him most dear ;
   Yet he will keep of her what is the true,
   His hasty deed in penitence undo,
Whereby in him the last dark savage strand
   Is struck from Nature, and his spirit new
Begs now to bear her to her own dear land.

CXII.

And many barbarous peoples thither flock
   From lands whereof no Greek hath yet a notion,
From East and West, from North new earth-born
     stock ;
   Around her now they roll in grand commotion,
   Yet in her find their soul's most sweet devotion ;
They come, they come from farthest bleakest
     Thule,
   Where her fair temples bind the edge of Ocean,
E'en from Atlantis where no King hath rule.

CXIII.

Europa's children seize the fleeting chance,
  To bring her home and to perfect their deed;
For they will hers and their own worth enhance,
  When they have to the full re-paid her meed,
  And in their fealty are ripe to bleed;
When placed again upon her ancient seat,
  She too hath won herself, is truly freed,
And they, completing her, themselves complete.

CXIV.

More ships at Tauris now are brought together
  Than in the olden time to Aulis came,
They had no stress of winds, had no foul weather;
  A greater act, to be of greater fame,
  Than hath been yet bound up with Helen's
    name;
And the new Gods send gales, not to take Troy,
  Not to avenge in hate a woman's shame,
Their will is to redeem, not to destroy.

CXV.

So act these men in noble gratitude
  To her who gave to them what was their best,
Who changed the jungled earth, the savage rude,
  Into a land and people that were blest,
  Obeying human law and God's behest;
But now the last and greatest deed is done,
  Return to Hellas is the final test
Whereby Greek and Barbarian are one.

CXVI.

Orestes, the mad Greek, his cure has found,
　The vengeful Furies him no more pursue;
Thoas, the wild Barbarian, is now sound,
　His jealous wrath is chastened into rue ;
　Both men are healed, begin their life anew,
Their hateful limit they will both erase,
　Both feel their oneness, have one thing to do,
Both sink down at her feet, and there embrace.

CXVII.

" Up, up !" a voice runs through the darkening
　　air,
　It is again the Hours, the watchful, true ;
" Up, up !" they sing with troubled note of care,
　" We shut and ope Olympus to the view,
　We guard the cloudy gate the Gods pass
　　through,
Now man they leave, the Fates and Furies
　throng ;
　Up, up ! there is the final deed to do ;
They come ! hark to the dread demonic song."

Iphigenia at Delphi.

Return and Restoration.

ARGUMENT.

The scene changes from Tauris back to Greece, to a place which may be called the Hellenic heart, namely, Delphi. First is heard the chorus of the Fates and Furies, the dark Powers of which Hellas is to be freed by the return of Iphigenia, who in the present Canto appears in two relations: first, alone and unrecognized; secondly, recognized and installed in her great vocation.

I. Upon the dark background of Fates and Furies there takes place a bright Greek festival, which brings together all the famous men who have returned from Troy, Nestor, Menelaus, Ulysses; the latter coming with Penelope. All celebrate their return from war and wandering.

In the midst of the festivity Iphigenia appears, alone and unknown to everybody. She catches the spirit of the time, and clearly sees what she is to do in her own land. She hears her old bard who once sang in Mycenæ (See First Canto). He sings the story of Achilles, the hero wrathful and reconciled, then he sings the fate of Agamemnon, and the woes of the House of Tantalus, to which she belongs. At last he sings her own tale of sacrifice, and utters the prophecy of her return. Iphigenia for a moment sinks in despair at the account of her bloody kinship, but soon rises up with new resolution.

Helen, too, comes to the Delphic festival, having been restored from Troy. Her great change is described.

(142)

A short account of her Trojan experience is given, and her internal struggles while in that city are indicated. She masters Aphrodite ere Troy can fall, and the Goddess herself changes with Helen. The bard comes forward and sings his second song in praise of Helen, which is in strong contrast with his former song. (First Canto.) He expresses his fervid desire for the one who has not yet returned, and Helen also feels deep longing for Iphigenia, when behold! she appears. (I—LXXXII.)

II. Recognition between the two women, the most different in character, yet belonging together. The people turn away from Helen to Iphigenia, and choose her for priestess of the new Apollo, who, though a God, has also been transformed from a Trojan divinity to a Hellenic one. With him the old Greek world is transformed into its true life and works. But scarce has this begun, when Thoas, the Taurian King, appears and tells what Iphigenia has done for Barbary. Through her deed too the Fates, who have always lowered over Greece, have been put to flight. After him Orestes, free of his madness, steps forth, and tells the story of his cure, whereby the Furies no longer pursue him. At the end of his declaration, the last song of the Fates and Furies is heard, vanishing from Delphi into the distance. Following it, is the new song of the Muses, which touches the final highest deed of Agamemnon's Daughter.

I.

" Around, around we circle hand in hand,
   We rule this Lower World, the Gods we rule,
We tie up Time itself within our band,
   The human Will is but our tiny tool,
   The man who fights against us is the fool,
In iron rim of fierce barbaric powers
   This little Greece we bind and press and pull ;
The man, the land, the God, e'en Zeus are ours."

II.

So sang the Fates, while they kept wheeling
      round
   In ever-closing curves the Delphic fane,
In wrath they beat the air, they smote the ground,
   Then tightly shut their triple grip again
   To rhythm of a wild tyrannic strain.
Blent in their song were heard the Furies too,
   Who screamed afar in vengeful sharp refrain
What they had done, and what they still would do:

III.

" Around we whirl in rage and strike and squirm,
 We gnash our fangs and scorn the note of bliss ;
We drop to earth and coil up like a worm,
 We crawl to that side now, and now to this,
 Our laugh is but a scoff, our speech a hiss,
We sway the man below, the Gods above
 Cannot the Furies from their rule dismiss ;
Our joy is pain and hate is what we love."

IV.

So sang the Furies, of themselves they sang,
 Around they whirled in rage and smote the
  ground,
They dropped into the dust and coiled and sprang,
 With snaky head upreared for sudden bound,
 Each serpent hair sent forth a hissing sound.
They mingled with the Fates — a dreadful
  throng ;
 The fixed Fates and frantic Furies found
A common hate and sang it in a song :

V.

" We too now with the Greeks to Delphi go,
 We triple Fates and Furies have control,
Together we one life in twain bestow,
 The outer world of man is ours, the whole,
 His inner world is ours, the very soul
Within the state of Greece, within the Greek ;
 We Fates the guilty deed on man shall roll,
We Furies then revenge on him shall wreak."

VI.

The strain arose from Delphic lands high-hilled,
  And flowed adown the slopes unto the dale,
The vineyards and the olive groves it filled,
  Where men and women echoed all the tale
  In far-heard notes that swung from height to
    vale,
They sang it at their work and at their feast,
  They hymned it to the beat of threshing flail,
And felt its awe from highest to the least.

VII.

From the Parnassian tops, where Muses played,
  Was floating over land and sea the lay
Of Fates and Furies to a world dismayed;
  It bubbled out of Castaly's bright play,
  And dimmed her lucent rill on all its way;
The Oracle could speak no other word
  Unto the multitude who came to pray,
And all their hearts were with it deeply stirred.

VIII.

O rocky Pytho, the one soul thou art
  Of this wide Grecian land and of the time;
Thou sendest thine own breath to every part,
  To touch the hidden chords of this fair clime,
  Whose thrill sets all the earth to thy deep chime;
From out thy mountain breast deep-cleft in twain,
  Speaks prophecy with freshest voice of prime,
And farthest Hellas hears the sacred strain.

IX.

Yet many years had Delphi lain untrod
  By heroes who were in the Trojan war ;
But now to land and family and God
  They had returned in spite of adverse star,
  And leaped the human and celestial bar ;
Again they gathered at the Delphic call,
  Which they had heard resounding near and far,
To come and hold a mighty festival.

X.

Those Grecian men were fain their grand return
  In that most sacred town to celebrate ;
They had no more in foreign land to yearn
  For wife and home, or haply to await
  On bloody bridge of war the blow of fate ;
A day of joy, yet not without a tear,
  For each had lost what Time could never mate ;
Again heroic shapes from Troy drew near.

XI.

The first was Nestor, aged man and wise,
  Whose snowy beard would brush the Delphic
    shrine,
As he unto the God gave sacrifice ;
  In burning Troy he saw the strifeful sign,
  And homeward fled at once across the brine ;
That city's fall was for his glance the end,
  He would not further probe the ways divine,
The will of Gods he sought not to transcend.

XII.

Next Spartan Menelaus thither came,
  Who wandered long, yet reached at last his
    home,
With Helen still his wife, but all men's fame;
  Far, far into the East he had to roam,
And cut a path unknown through salty foam;
When he the wiles of Proteus had outdone,
  And through old Egypt's mystic land had
    come,
He caught beneath all changing forms the One.

XIII.

Ulysses, too, at Delphi now appears,
  Though his return was greatest of them all,
He fought and wandered homeward twenty years,
  He saw strange lands and beings magical,
  With giants strove, who sought him to enthrall,
He passed the Underworld of ghostly forms,
  Where all the shades gave answer to his call,
Then back to home on earth outrode the storms.

XIV.

He was the man who pried below, above;
  The dear Unknown he made his daily guest,
With the Impossible he was in love,
  Beyond the ken of men he took his test;
  With bold emprise he plunged into the West,
Whose far domains he first of mortals trod,
  Yet on the bound of worlds he could not rest,
He sought to burst the limit of the God.

XV.

O Chian voice, could I to mine but tell
    As thou to thine his wondrous tale hast told,
Again would flow the deep Pierian well
    In which are seen the ages to unfold;
    All Time would move as I my leaves unrolled,
And out my lines would step the man to-day,
    Who to my music would the world uphold:
But stop — mine is another tale — away.

XVI.

With him his wife had come, Penelope,
    Hers was the steadfast heart, most loyal, true;
Yet prudence joined she to fidelity,
    She kept her husband's home and country too,
    Whereby he ever could return anew;
Well she deserved with him the equal part
    Of honor now to the most honored due —
The wisest head had paired the truest heart.

XVII.

So gathered round the fane the heroes great,
    Now old and full of silent suffering,
To hear the past, their deeds to celebrate,
    Some little joy into their lives to bring,
    And dull awhile the point of sorrow's sting;
Their days were full of deep-remembered pain,
    Though they had taken Troy and slain its king,
And had returned to land and home again.

XVIII.

And e'en the Delphic God was one of those
Who out the East to Hellas had returned ;
Apollo smote in Troy the Greeks as foes,
 The God had not the trend of Time discerned,
 Yet through his error he his wisdom learned,
He, though a God, transformed his vast mistake,
 Whereby he had a new devotion earned ;
Him, wisest God, the Greeks will not forsake.

XIX.

Fair maidens soon attuned the merry song,
 And interwove sweet sounds into the dance,
While in their steps the Graces tripped along,
 At whose dear shapes the eye falls in a trance,
 And to a music seen is blent each glance ;
A stream of mounted youths then overfills
 The rolling slopes which seem with steeds to
  prance ;
Far the procession tosses mid the hills.

XX.

Soft flutes and frantic timbrels mingle joy,
 And fling on breathing air life's anodyne ;
Where now have vanished all the ills of Troy?
 Ah, woe the word ! what darker, deeper line
 That in the joyful strain doth intertwine !
Of Fates and Furies still breaks out the hymn,
 To jar the song around the fane divine,
While o'er the Graces hover goblins grim :

XXI.

" Forget us not, we too are in the song,
  Within each Grecian voice and soul we dwell
We circle round about each Grecian throng,
  Upon this merry world we cast our spell,
  And Time the echo is of what we tell. —
Hist, Hist ! A foe we scent on Delphic air,
  Low-sounding up the vale we hear a knell,
A stranger draweth near, beware, beware."

XXII.

The joyous festival had well begun,
  When lo ! a woman moves around the hill,
And enters Delphi in the morning sun;
  She walks up to the clear Castalian rill,
  And drinks of it and hears its sweetest trill;
She turns to pass into the town above ;
  But first in a deep glance she standeth still,
Then slowly moves into the sacred grove.

XXIII.

Who is the lady of the look unknown?
  Iphigenia — she without delay
From port of Aulis had set out alone,
  Where she had landed only yesterday,
  And where again a thousand vessels lay,
Tall ships of Barbary, which there did bring
  Her with Orestes o'er the watery way;
The leader Thoas was, the Taurian King.

XXIV.

Her name none knew, or how she came, or when;
  Nor made she haste her lineage to say,
She flitted through the surging crowds of men,
  From every side she heard the bodeful lay
  Of Fates and Furies pierce the holiday;
In every deed entwined their lurid song,
  Which shot dark threads through colors bright
      and gay,
Yet had their counterpart in all the throng.

XXV.

Her sorrow rose when she that song had heard
  Tinge with its discord all the Delphic dale,
Nor could she to herself suppress the word:
  " I see at home these monsters still prevail
  Which once I saw far Barbary assail;
But there they are put down and sway no more;
  My Hellas hath beneath its joy a wail,
It is not what it seemed to me before.

XXVI.

" I hear but of the vengeful sack of Troy,
  The many men and women slaved or slain;
The spirit everywhere is to destroy,
  Such deeds, I know, leave tinct in man their
      grain,
  What he hath done, comes back to him again,
The city burnt a wraith of vengeance hath
  Which the mad victor's heart will rend amain
And him will smite in turn with his own wrath.

XXVII.

" I see that in my land I have again to do
   What I at Tauris with the years have done,
To give my spirit's offering anew,
      Change vengeful father to the gentle son ;
   Another Troy must on this soil be won,
Not by fierce arms or furious conflagration,
      All Troy, the East and West, must be made one
In helpful deed with the Hellenic nation."

XXVIII.

So moved the woman lone among the Greeks,
   By men unrecognized in her own land ;
To learn the story of the time she seeks,
      From all she hears of Agamemnon's band,
   The mighty deed done on the Trojan strand,
The valor bursting red in streams of blood ;
      She feels the war-beat to a fever fanned,
As round each singer men admiring stood.

XXIX.

But soon she caught the fragment of a strain
   That waved the air more mellow than the rest,
And as she neared the spot, it swelled again,
      And sounded, as it sweetly rose, more blest ;
   She stood and looked from a small hilly crest,
Above the shoulders of the listening crowd ;
      She saw an ancient bard, from whose deep
         breast
The tender notes were welling clear and loud.

XXX.

It was the bard who in Mycenæ sang
  Long since when she was but a little maid;
His deep bass-voice had now a melting pang,
    Round his great thoughts the nimble fancies
      played,
    As his white beard on toying breezes strayed ;
His wingéd words agleam would flit the air,
    Like long thin cloudlets through the welkin
      frayed,
Was twirled in passing wind his blanchéd hair.

XXXI.

Thus looked and sang that bard Meonides,
  Who hymned so well the famous Trojan woe,
Who knew fatality in all degrees,
    As it was stamped on men long, long ago ;
    Like him, this singer too had felt the blow
Of deep-dispensing Gods, for he was blind;
    Yet deeper, purer was the inner flow,
As he the world more clearly saw in mind.

XXXII.

She glided through the crowd and heard the song ;
  It sang the wrath which stirred Achilles dread,
When he rose up against a Grecian wrong
    Done by the King who was the Army's head,
    That wrongful King, it was her father dead ;
The Ruler and the Hero caused the strife,
    Whereby not they, but their true people bled,
And many a gallant chieftain lost his life.

XXXIII.

Ah, fateful, furious was that song of wrath,
  The words of blood poured out the deeds of
    blood !
But a far deeper note the singer hath,
  Which sang Achilles imaging the good,
  Forgiving to his foes in tender mood;
The Hero true she saw in him arise,
  Not by the cruel deed, but brotherhood;
It was the image of her sacrifice.

XXXIV.

Great was her joy, when in her low disguise
  She heard her act wind through the Hero's lot,
How he to vision of her life did rise,
  Though oftentimes she was by him forgot,
  And he in mad revenge would slay and plot;
Still he would soon bethink himself again,
  The Leader he forgave, and then would not
Slay Priam old for dear Patroclus slain.

XXXV.

The singer struck a newer, sadder strain,
  The piteous tale of Agamemnon's fate,
How he at home by his own wife was slain,
  How she her hearth with lust did desecrate;
  The story on the daughter's heart-strings ate,
Of her own mother and her father sung
  To all assembled Greeks, both small and great :
Her lips turned pale and down her head she hung :

XXXVI.

"Ye Gods ! the mighty Leader of the Greeks
Is butchered like an ox within its stall !
Return to home he hath not, which he seeks ;
Instead of it he hears death's sudden call
Just as he steps into his palace hall ;
Return is not for him from Trojan strife,
Revenge, not Love, sits on Mycenæ's wall,
With broken vows that lap the blood of life.

XXXVII.

" O mother, mother, what a great mistake
For thee and me thy vengeful lesson was ;
Thou boldly slewest husband for my sake,
And yet I was not dead, thou hadst no cause
To overturn the deity's last laws ;
Thus err we, when we take into our hands
The justice which the Gods without our flaws,
In foresight far, dispense to men and lands."

XXXVIII.

More deeply still sobbed Agamemnon's daughter :
" Then such am I, and of such parents born,
Of parents' parents slain in kindred slaughter !
Methinks till now I never felt forlorn ;
Oh might I never see to-morrow morn !
Can I now change ancestral bloody strands,
Release from Furies' fang the bosom torn,
Oh can I whiten still these gory hands ! "

XXXIX.

The bard began a milder lay to sing,
  Which soothed with tender notes her hapless
    pain,
It was the lay of her own offering
  At Aulis by the sea, where she was slain,
  Yet saved, that she might do her deed again ;
Lost Helen's restoration there she earned,
  And freedom gave to clear the guilty stain ;
By her deed, too, the Greek has now returned.

XL.

The song's deep solace bore her in its flood,
  She felt that she had stemmed her house's guilt,
And stanched the ever-flowing stream of blood,
  Which, in the time of old Thyestes spilt,
  Had stained each kindred sword from point to
    hilt ;
But yet more deeply ran the tuneful word :
  A new Greek world, by her to be now built,
Had to prophetic strain the poet stirred :

XLI.

" I yet shall touch her with this aged hand,
  For I have heard in truth she is not dead,
But is still living in a far-off land,
  That she on Dian's altar never bled,
  But by the Goddess she away was led,
Until the strifeful Trojan time be past,
  And Helen be to home returned who fled ;
Then will she too return to Greece, the last.

XLII.

" This last return will be the greatest, best;
To end of Time she will in Hellas stay ;
I have deep faith it is the God's behest,
    That she no longer shall remain away,
    Who gave herself for all upon that day;
And some great blessing she will with her bring,
    When to Apollo's fane she comes to pray,
And bears anew to us her offering.

XLIII.

" She cannot long be absent from us still,
    I feel the very point of time draw near
When she, in coming home, will all fulfill,
    And in this Delphic seat she will appear,
    Led by the love of her own people dear;
All have returned but her, e'en the lost wife,
    Methinks that she already must be here,
This day, this spot is telling of her life."

XLIV.

She listened to her piteous fate, but kept
    Within distressful heart the bursting sigh;
Yet inwardly at her own tale she wept,
    A lonely tear would wander to her eye,
    The silent herald of her sympathy.
She seemed to think it was another's lot,
    When she beheld the maid at Aulis die;
That she the sufferer was, she quite forgot.

XLV.

O woman, woman! O thou image truest
 Which sorrow moulds in its long painful stress;
Only to be compassionate thou knewest,
 Thou didst not know it was thine own distress
 That touched thy soul of self-forgetfulness;
On thee comes back thy pity's overflow,
 Which always through another must thee bless,
Een that thou art not dead thou scarce dost know.

XLVI.

Yet one fixed mystery she could not break,
 She saw that she a guilt untold had brought
On one who was mistaken for her sake;
 Her death to quit, the darkest crime was
  wrought;
 That crime was done but for a phantom thought;
For her she saw a father slain, a mother stained,
 Fate seemed at last to have her life-thread
  caught,
In voiceless woe unto herself she plained:

XLVII.

" Of being's source to be the enemy,
 The fateful child to be, though innocent,
Through whom both parents guilty are and die —
 It wraps the Gods in deep bewilderment.
 O why have I been darkly hither sent?
It is the Fates who turn on me their power:
 To their decree I shall at last be bent,
They come and I must yield — it is their hour.

XLVIII.

" I too must be a link of that long chain
Which hangs from Tantalus, and ever will;
To slay mine own and by them to be slain,
Is the last law which I must too fulfill.
—No, no; 'tis madness; I shall conquer still,
Transform my birth into a source of good,
I destiny shall whelm into my will,
And guilt of Tantalids cleanse from my blood."

XLIX.

But hark! a fiendish laughter scoffs the air
Yet mingled with a wild demoniac pain;
Just as the words drop from the woman there
The Fates and Furies howl and hiss again:
" Forget us not, we sing the Delphic strain;
See! another woman comes with demons' powers!
Here still our ancient realm we shall main-
tain,
The fane, the God, the woman too is ours."

L.

Meanwhile the crowd rushed to the wall to gaze
Far down the slope, beyond the Delphic dale,
Till where the blue Corinthian waters raise
On gentle throbbing waves the nodding sail,
Or heave on high the reeling bark more frail;
The silvery sparkle flashes into view,
Or traces out a momentary trail,
Then vanishes into the billows blue.

11

LI.

Above those azure pulses of the deep,
  Uprearing from the valley rose a train,
It slowly curled about the mountain steep
    Through pointed rocks athwart its pathway
      lain,
    At times it seemed to grapple might and main,
As if in mortal wrestle with the way,
  Which showed a fierce resistance, but in vain;
The line kept creeping up, and made no stay.

LII.

When it had reached at last the Delphic gate,
  It seemed to turn upon itself and think,
As if it for a time did hesitate,
    Standing alone with doubt on some deep brink,
    Which for a moment made the courage sink;
It would not enter in the sacred wall,
  Smit by some sudden scruple it did shrink,
Or fear again a hidden guilt or fall.

LIII.

But yielding soon it came into the town,
  For many voices shouted strong request,
It marched in still procession up and down,
    All flocked to see who was the newest guest,
    They marked one shape far more than all the
      rest,
The dame with penitential, downcast eye,
  Which told the sorrowing tale of years unblest;
She never once looked up as she passed by.

LIV.

Helen it was, who had from Troy returned,
  Once more in her old Spartan home she dwelt,
The deepest lesson of the world had learned,
  The sharpest pang of human life had felt,
  The fiercest blow to her own land had dealt,
And to her spouse, though he had all forgiven ;
  She came to the shrine of Artemis and knelt
And looked up in her face, with rue heart-riven.

LV.

The heroes then could not restrain the tear
  At such great beauty to such sorrow bound;
They wept for her, their image still most dear,
  And for themselves, who such distress had
    found,
  And left so many friends cold in Troy's ground ;
Fell Memory shot deep into the heart
  The look of brothers slain, or starved, or
    drowned,
And in themselves they felt the deathly dart.

LVI.

The mighty multitude of people wept,
  It would have broken up the festival,
If fairest Helen had not forward stepped,
  And gave her drug which men Nepenthe call ;
  At once it soothed the sorrows of them all,
At her sweet look they soon forgot their pain,
  In her they saw the rise out of the fall,
Great was the loss, but greater still the gain.

LVII.

The tender lines of hidden suffering
  Wove all their saddest story through her face,
But round them other lines did gently cling,
    Which would the sharp, remorseful thought
      erase,
    And softly write forgiveness there and grace;
So could she quench the very grief she made,
    Though trouble gone would leave for proof its
      trace;
The guilt had fled, but still had left its shade.

LVIII.

Out of her life there shone calm penitence,
  With steadfast will her deed yet to atone;
Though never more she could have innocence,
    She still had something won for what was gone
    That to remorse she was not left alone;
She had for error won the compensation,
    She knew the thorny way, the heart-torn moan,
And through the lapse she knew the restoration.

LIX.

In Troy already she had often tried
  Her heavy lot of servitude to flee,
In agony of self-reproach she cried
    That Aphrodite's thrall she would not be,
    Yet could herself not of the Goddess free.
She fought within, the Grecians fought without,
    To save her and themselves to liberty;
Both of their struggles were a ten years' doubt.

LX.

Once Aphrodite to her chamber came,
When Paris had been slain, her Trojan spouse,
And she had willed henceforth to cleanse her
    blame ;
The Goddess sought desire again to rouse,
That it might snap afresh her holy vows,
And promised youth's sweet victory anew,
    With every potent charm Love's zone endows,
Would give a young heroic husband too.

LXI.

The Goddess tried her far away to lure,
To distant East, to curse of Babylon,
Where she would have no struggle to endure;
    Where she could lie forever in the sun
    Which showed no guilt, no deed to be undone.
But she resisted all that blandishment,
    She did the temple of the Goddess shun,
And to her soul's own trysting-place she went.

LXII.

Yet Memnon found her once, the son of Morn,
    And prayed that he might bear her to the day,
Far in the Orient where he was born,
    And with him there to shine the early ray
    Which lightly wakes the world in jocund play ;
But she refused, she would return to Greece,
    Back to her home would walk the thorny way,
And there work out in sorrow her release.

LXIII.

Then Memnon left, he was the last of all,
  Most brave, most beautiful of Troy's array;
At once he dashed out of the Trojan wall,
  And fighting fell upon that very day,
  Foreknowing well what in the battle lay;
As he breathed out his breath, that hour Troy fell,
  Its soul was dead and in him passed away,
The Gods departed from its citadel.

LXIV.

The Greeks rushed in the gate, the city burned,
  The people and the aged king they slew;
Whom once Achilles' wrath had spared, they
    spurned,
  The captives' prayer they would not listen to,
  The cry of babes no tear of pity drew.
Vengeance they show with all its rage unblest,
  Nor think that they shall suffer what they do,
By waking Furies fierce in their own breast.

LXV.

The Greeks erelong the wretched Helen found,
  They bore her hastily into a tent,
With hands and feet in triple cordage bound,
  And in their wrath at once they would have
    sent
  Her soul to Hades for its punishment;
But holy Calchas said: " It must not be,
  She hath a spirit new, a new intent,
And of her guilty life she now is free.

LXVI.

" She hath her evil deed in full undone,
She is renewed by her contrition deep,
And her young days of blamelessness hath won ;
Troy could no longer changed Helen keep,
Yet with her lost it lies a burning heap;
Home she will now return without a stain,
Though often she the past distress beweep,
She is restored, is Helen once again."

LXVII.

So spake the priest of her mid blazing Troy.
But now she comes to seek the Delphic fane,
To have a share of all that tearful joy,
A share of the great loss and greater gain,
Of all those sad returns to learn the bane,
To learn the blessing which doth renovate,
And Phœbus too, returned, to greet again,
Beholding e'en a God regenerate.

LXVIII.

The way to Delphi ran beside the sea,
Which gently rose and seemed to stroke the
shrine
Of Aphrodite, Love's fair deity;
There Helen once beheld the form divine,
And from the lightning heard a voice malign
Commanding her to cross to Troy the wave:
But now the Goddess showed a milder sign,
And spake in tones subdued these speeches grave :

LXIX.

"O Helen, I, the Goddess, must confess,
 In thy self-conquest thou hast conquered me;
In thy great struggle felt I mine own stress,
 And now I feel that I must change with thee,
 Or yield to time and pale mortality.
My Trojan home doth lie a ruined heap,
 Ah me! what shall I do henceforth to be?
My ancient throne I can no longer keep.

LXX.

"With all the Gods I have old Troy to leave,
 The spirit new into my life instil;
Yet I must not me of myself bereave,
 Love must not perish, Love I can be still,
 Though all transfigured with another will,
Which binds the family in its sweet grace,
 Whence Love shall flow till it the world shall fill,
And reaching up, it shall the Gods embrace."

LXXI.

The voice had ceased, but left a vision strange,
 Upon which Helen all her journey thought:
"The God has then along with man to change,
 To be the God who man has truly taught,
 To be the spirit of the spirit sought,
From whom eternally the transformation
 Into the man and world is overwrought,
Whereby the God is one in all mutation."

LXXII.

So Argive Helen came through guilt to thought;
  The bottom of her mystery to find
By looking deep into herself she sought;
  But quickly out the reaches of her mind
  The thought would flit, and leave all dark be-
  hind.
Still glimpses flashed through mystic meditation,
  Of one whose love of self took in her kind,
Whereby she saw her own in man's salvation.

LXXIII.

There Helen stands amid the Grecian throng,
  More beautiful she seemeth than before,
She shows the depths revealing struggles long;
  Not youthful bloom, which they did once adore,
  But all the wealth that flows from Time's rich
  store
Seems now to lie within her graven face,
  Whose melting lines would tremble evermore,
And tender throbs would follow every trace.

LXXIV.

Again the Grecian heroes gather round,
  Her to behold, with worship in the heart;
In her new look is healed the last old wound,
  Each knows himself to be of her a part;
  He, too, of destiny had felt the dart
For sharing in the guilt of Trojan life,
  Yet was a wiser man for all the smart
When he to harmony returned from strife.

LXXV.

Then came the bard with harp and tuneful voice,
   Began to touch the sure responsive string,
Which with his note would weep or would rejoice;
   He, too, had been at Troy and felt the sting,
   He knew the triumph and the suffering;
He, too, had thence returned, in deed and song;
   His deep-changed strain he now began to sing,
As he stood up before her in the throng:

LXXVI.

" O Helen, I am old, and I am blind,
   My human strength, I feel, is nearly spent;
But I have left in clearer sight my mind,
   Thee to behold still supereminent,
   And see new glories in thy beauty blent;
Thou hast preserved all of thine ancient treasures,
   And to them pain and gain of life hast lent;
Fair thou art now beyond my Grecian measures.

LXXVII.

" I sang thy youth in wildest strains of youth,
   Into my line I put thy precious bloom,
Thy beauty was for me the highest truth,
   For aught but thee the world had not the
      room;
I knew not then the silent spreading doom
Which over thee and over me was hung,
   That we must march not to, but through the
      tomb,
Return alive once more, though old, yet young.

LXXVIII.

" O might I see again what once I saw,
  The hill and sky and sea, the Earth's sweet
    flower!
Behold thee beautiful without a flaw,
  And feel thee flash into my sight the power
Whose spell into a moment fleets the hour!
My Grecian clime without mine eye is cold,
  It seemeth to have lost Time's fairest dower;
O Helen, I am blind and I am old.

LXXIX.

" But I must stop the Muse of aged regret,
  And sing what recompense the Gods bestow:
The senses' wilder rapture is now let,
  The sunset calm, but not the sunrise glow
Is mine; the less I see, the more I know;
Now might I build of thy return the lay;
  I sing no more the battle's overthrow,
The ecstasy of joy, or love's light play.

LXXX.

" I have returned, my song has too returned,
  In tender mood from furious Trojan vein;
It has in thine its own new world discerned,
  And tunes to thy deep soul its inward strain,
That the great loss doth bring the greater gain;
And all these Grecians have returned with thee,
  Not over Troy we chant the loud refrain,
But over our own selves the victory.

LXXXI.

" But there is one whom I still deeply miss,
    The one who gave herself that Hellas be,
Whom as a little maid I oft would kiss,
    When at the hearth she sat upon my knee,
    And listened rapt to childhood's minstrelsy;
The consecrated one of all, I say,
    She too must home return as well as we,
Return to feast with us this very day."

LXXXII.

Out of the multitude then Helen moved;
    She felt upholden by the bard's strong word,
And all its truth in her own bosom proved;
    Yet she too felt the selfsame loss which stirred
    Him to the tender tuneful plaint she heard,
Till sense of loss turned one still cry for her
    Who always gave herself for those who erred,
But in her own life never once did err.

LXXXIII.

So tender flowed the thoughts of that high dame
    That from them fell to earth a tearful dew;
Unto the border of the throng she came,
    There she beheld a face she thought she knew,'
    She stopped, astonished at the sudden view,
As if she saw a spirit on the air;
    And when her stricken speech she could renew,
She spake unto that face before her there:

LXXXIV.

" Iphigenia, my hope, hast thou returned?
And with the other weeping Greeks art here?
For thee alone we all just now have yearned,
    And yet my sense of sight I have to fear —
Mine eye doth paint thy picture on its tear ;
Returned thou hast from a much further land
    Than Troy, I ween; from Hades drawest near,
Once more to make complete our earthly band.

LXXXV.

" Ah yes, thou hast returned whence none return,
    Thou art the shade my longing makes of thee ;
Thy life on earth to live I daily burn ;
    But thou hast burst the last captivity,
And wilt no more the tomb's dark vassal be ;
Thou hast returned, I hear thy highest call,
    Now first I feel that I am truly free,
Thou hast returned from death, to save us all."

LXXXVI.

She spake the hintful words, yet scarcely durst
    Draw near and touch in love the ghostly hand ;
Yet Helen was of all the Greeks the first
    To know the priestess strange in her own land,
What lay in her return to understand ;
Of womanhood the twain most different —
    Yet in one plan complete they were both
        planned,
Two lives in one great providence were blent.

LXXXVII.

The one through deepest fall could highest rise,
    And from her stain become again unstained;
The other rose through perfect sacrifice,
    Without the fall she stainless aye remained;
    Yet each of them her own true good attained,
Each only through the other grew complete,
    Both sides were one, in thought divine con-
        tained;
Now speaks the seeming ghost in language meet:

LXXXVIII.

" I am the same and I was never slain,
    To Lower Hades I have yet to go,
Where dark Proserpine has her sunless reign;
    Yet through one Hades I have passed in woe,
    I have come back to tell you what I know;
In far barbaric world has been my stay,
    Where I was borne divinely long ago,
When I at Aulis vanished out the day.

LXXXIX.

" But tell, what sad yet happy time is this,
    Wherein ye make the noble festival?
I feel the sorrow mingled in the bliss,
    A mellow joy that ripens from the fall,
    A gain that doth its very pain recall;
A melting change flows out the common heart,
    Ye noble Greeks have bled at Troy for all,
But the old wound is healed a better part.

XC.

" I think now of another holiday,
  The last I saw in high Mycenæ's hall,
When Paris thither bent his doomful way,
  And every Grecian soul he made his thrall,
  Who in the glances of his eye might fall;
Yet would I not a single person name,
  We all were blind, the guilt belonged to all,
And to the Gods we all have paid the blame.

XCI.

" But now we are restored to Greece at last,
  Though while we sing with joy, we have to
    weep,
For with us we have brought all of the past:
  What we have won, we shall forever keep,
  And the full harvest of our sorrows reap;
Here shall we gather on Apollo's hill,
  Where rests the sacred sun upon the steep,
And harmony flows down the Muses' rill."

XCII.

From Helen, then, the people turn away,
  And Helen turns, with her new look of love,
As to some sky-descended God to pray,
  Whose lofty presence fills the sacred grove;
  To Iphigenia all the people move,
They seek to near the center of their life,
  Attuned to that new music from above,
Transfigured to her spirit out of strife.

XCIII.

They choose her priestess of Apollo's fane,
    The oracle she will henceforth declare;
The double word she will to men explain,
    Of breath divine she also hath a share;
    She will inform with speech the Delphic air,
And add thereto a measure musical;
    The true Hellenic spirit everywhere
She feels, the first, then speaks it clear to all.

XCIV.

In her the new Apollo finds his speech,
    Not he who once against the Greeks did fight,
But he who will his faithful people teach
    The word of wisdom and the deed of right;
    He hath become the God of inner light,
Transformed from outer sheen of Eastern sun;
    When back to Hellas turned his glances bright,
Another character divine he won.

XCV.

As once the self-same God in daily toil
    Served King Admetus of fair Thessaly,
And labored like a bondman of the soil,
    Till of himself he wrought a being free,
    And rose therefrom into a deity;
So now the servile Trojan time is past,
    To which the Grecian God was held in fee;
He has with other Greeks returned at last.

XCVI.

With him, too, all at Delphi was transformed,
The very stones sprang into temples rare,
And by a soul divine within were warmed,
    Each block sought in itself to be the fair
    White fane, which perfect rose upon the air;
To music sweet the shapeless forms were trimmed,
    All marched in place out of their rocky lair,
While lofty old Parnassus to them hymned.

XCVII.

And helpless marble at a touch would spring
    Into life-seeming shapes of look divine:
The Muses, who the sweetest strain could sing,
    Apollo who from stone began to shine,
    And chant his Delphic lay with Sisters nine.
Forth Gods would start at Artist's strong command;
    He only smote with chisel on a line,
But had a heart-stroke beating from his hand.

XCVIII.

There is the transformation, too, of man
    To one who looks before and looks behind,
Who in himself doth past and future scan,
    Pours all the vasty world into his mind,
    And cannot rest till in it truth he find;
Who trains his body, too, until it be
    The semblance beautiful of all mankind,
Revealed in games and dance and poesy.

12

XCIX.

The Gods too were transformed in that great time,
    Bursting the bound that everywhere had stood,
They upwards rose into Olympian prime,
    Cast off the ugly form of idol rude,
    Which could but show the brand of finitude;
That was the happy hour they were set free,
    They passed from lust to love, from greed to
        good,
From red revenge they turned to charity.

C.

And Delphi was the lofty seat thereof,
    The bringer of the mighty transformation,
Which came to earth and man and Gods above,
    It was of all the world a new creation,
    Whose fragrance sweetest fell on that Greek
        nation;
The priestess now was borne into her place,
    To bring about the final restoration,
Which would the Greek unite with all his race.

CI.

But see! what new procession at the gate?
    It moves with stately march into the fane,
And at its head a man of royal state:
    Thoas it is, the king with all his train,
    In vesture tinct with many-shaded grain,
Not in white play of Grecian fold on fold,
    Whose simple ripple flows without a stain,
But decked in shifting hues and shining gold.

CII.

Soon in the train the swell of music rose
  In many a blending tone and winding turn,
Which leaped up with the joys, dropped with the
    woes,
  As they in human feeling wordless burn,
  Or can, unsatisfied with speech, but yearn;
Then voices rose together in a cry
  Of suffering, or song of struggle stern,
Woven in fancies bright of minstrelsy.

CIII.

And mighty bards were in that lordly train,
  Who there began to chant around the king,
In measures new, a strange enraptured strain,
    Whose very words would climb and kiss and
    cling,
    Yet in a melody were ever vanishing
Out of the world of sight to realms unseen,
  As they would hymn the noble offering,
Which made the stream of time flow down more
    clean.

CIV.

The Greeks looked on that King in wonderment,
  All what they were he was, yet he was more;
Unto their Art Humanity he lent,
  The deepest love he joined to widest lore,
  In him the Graces gave to worth their store,
In him had vanished quite the gentile hate,
  Barbarian now he would the Greek restore,
The bound of nations was for him no fate.

CV.

They asked him from what region he had come,
  Whence he such wisdom in his life had learned;
Was it the gathered treasures of his home,
  Or of some other land where people burned
  To find what knowledge sought, what virtue
    earned?
He was a Greek, yet Greek beyond their ken,
  In him a brother they indeed discerned,
Yet not to them alone, but to all men.

CVI.

To queries yet unspoken, Thoas spake :
  "This priestess is the one who hath us taught
And all our world the spirit's bond to break;
  She came to us a sacrifice unsought,
  When she to the altar was a victim brought
By her own people ; still the Taurians say,
  An image fell from heaven, that hath wrought
Us to herself by her long priestly stay.

CVII.

" She hath the wild barbarian conquered,
  Not by the vengeance of a Trojan war ;
The savage world she hath in triumph led,
  But not enchainéd to a prisoner's car ;
  No city sacked, no town in blackened char,
Doth mark her path like ghostly skeleton ;
  She to her soul hath changed the Near and Far,
And freedom for a prisoned world hath won.

CVIII.

" Now she hath come to save her own fair land,
  As she hath saved already Barbary;
Home I have brought her with this grateful band,
  I see no more in Greek an enemy,
  The surest sign whereof is, Here am I.
Her sacrifice henceforth the Greeks must show,
  And from revenge live unto charity,
Which out the bosom doth the Furies throw.

CIX.

" When Greeks have blotted out their spirit's
    bound
  Which them from Barbary doth separate,
They have the holy medicine then found,
  Which will forever cure their sickly state,
  By taking off that outer world of Fate;
And when the Furies out their breast they cast,
  Pursuing men no more in vengeful hate,
The Furies, too, will cease pursuit at last."

CX.

At this strong regal word, forth from the train
  Orestes stepped, in presence magical;
On Delphic sacred ground he stood again,
  From which he once had fled and leaped the
    wall,
  And ran with horrid cries funereal,
By snaky Furies down the rocks pursued,
  Till he to Tauris had obeyed the call:
Now of the monsters freed, he calmly stood.

CXI.

All Greece had seen his spell and pitied him,
 Yet for his ransom knew not what to do;
For Greeks themselves were prey to vengeance
  grim,
 As well as he, they needed pity too;
 And now, when they beheld Orestes new,
They could not think that he was truly cured;
 Near to his tranquil countenance they drew,
And then by word and touch themselves assured.

CXII.

It was a time of wild astonishment;
 Orestes to their thousand queries said:
" For wise Apollo's sister, Artemis, I went;
 I trailed the mighty sea to Tauris dread,
 For so the God's deep oracle I read;
There in a fane was spoke the flaming word,
 Whose light at once me out of madness led,
When I in my dark trance the priestess heard.

CXIII.

" First from that speech myself I truly learned,
 I rose renewed, and looked in vision free;
My thought flashed forward, backward, in me
  burned,
 Till all the circling deed I seemed to see
 Take in the past, take in futurity.
I saw the vengeance which man wreaks on man
 Turn back on him, and the avenger be;
His curse on others is but his own ban.

CXIV.

" That priestess strange I found to be my sister,
  Whom I, perturbed, knew not, but deemed as
  dead,
Since that dark day the Greeks at Aulis missed her
  From Dian's temple, whither she was led.
This is the sister whom the God instead
Of stony idol means to be adored ;
  Through her the fangéd Furies from me fled,
With her restored, am I and you restored."

CXV.

His word was done, but hark! what gnashing
  throng
  In maddened wind which out of Delphi blows!
And in that wind is heard a wailing song
  Which weaker, weaker in the distance grows,
  Yet wrathful still, as strain of dying foes.
The pang of banishment that voice doth wring,
  And with it other voices mingle woes;
List, list! Again the Fates and Furies sing :

CXVI.

" Farewell, O lovely Delphi, our last seat !
  O Hellas dear, our ancient home, farewell !
The bitter hour has come for our retreat,
  In Thoas' word we Fates have heard our knell,
  The outer world we can no more compel ;
Since Barbary hath changed its hate to love,
  We can no longer lay on man our spell;
Away ! we rule no more the Gods above."

CXVII.

" Farewell, O lovely Delphi, our last seat !
  O Hellas dear, our ancient home farewell !
The bitter hour has come for our retreat,
    We Furies now have heard Orestes tell
    The deadly tale which tolls to us our knell ;
From out our clutch he has regained his soul,
    The inner world we can no more compel,
Away ! man is now free of our control."

CXVIII.

" Farewell, O lovely Delphi, our last seat !
  O Hellas dear, our ancient home farewell !
The bitter hour has come for our retreat !"
    Thus parting strains of Fates and Furies fell
    Faintly, then faintly rose in dying swell :
" The bitter hour has come for our retreat !
    O Hellas dear, our ancient home, farewell !
Farewell, O lovely Delphi, our last seat !"

CXIX.

Behind the Delphic mountain soon they sank,
  Into its caverns deep they darkly sped ;
Castalian waters they no longer drank,
    Nor threatened happy Delphi overhead ;
    The holy priestess has them banishéd,
Where still by mountain dwarfs they are adored ;
    For Fates and Furies are not wholly dead,
Though Agamemnon's daughter be restored.

CXX.

But now in Delphi breathes another strain,
  Which rises out the rill of Castaly,
And sings through vines and olive groves again,
  With its sweet cadence wreathes the farthest
    sea;
It is the joyous strain of Muses, free
From savage monsters, which did them affray;
  For with the priestess won they liberty,
And thus they hymned her and themselves that
    day:

CXXI.

" Now hast thou made thy deed, thyself complete;
  Not till thou didst remove man's narrow bound,
Could we in song thine own fair freedom greet;
  Thy brother's limits must thine own be found,
  Thou shalt not stand, till he rise from the
    ground;
In freeing him, thou art thyself set free,
  Thy sacrifice hath to thyself come round,
And through another hath perfected thee.

CXXII.

" We sing thine Aulian, Taurian, Delphic deed;
  Done for the sake of Greek and all mankind;
But in the deed thou hast received the meed,
  Thou art now whole in character and mind,
  Thou and the world one harmony designed,
Of human life thou hast well won the height,
  All in thyself, thyself in all dost find,
And show what man will be in his own right.

CXXIII.

" Not thou alone, all are to be made whole,
　　Each man is to become thine image true,
And in his own reflect thy perfect soul,
　　As thou hast done, will he forever do.
　　Yet to us rises a still vaster view:
The nations shall renounce for one another,
　　Therein like thee, shall win their freedom too,
When each shall look on each as its own brother."

CXXIV.

Such strains rose out the fount where Muses dwell,
　　Last herald of the newer minstrelsy ;
The perfect image floating in their well
　　Did rise and walk in sight of mortal eye,
　　Clad in the vesture Time shall on it try,
Transfigured into music and sweet grace ;
　　And all therein the mightier semblance could
　　　　descry :
The man's, the nation's, and the world's one face.

Iphigenia.

BIBLIOGRAPHICAL.

The foregoing poem, first published in 1885, has been out of the book market for some years. As it has won a few friends — enough of them apparently to keep it alive a while yet — who still speak of it occasionally, and ask after it, the book may be said to have acquired a certain right of resuscitation. Accordingly it appears again, with a small but bright spark of hope in its heart, dreaming that it may have another period of new life, in which to gain some more friends.

Here the confession must be made that the former opportunity of the book was not the best. The first edition was badly printed, being the work of a foreign printer, who united excellent intentions with a small knowledge of English. Then the proof-reader was not a good one, being myself; but proof-reading became paralyzed when the correction was pretty certain to be the means of introducing a new mistake into the types. Several times I have had the vexation of seeing critical objections to the poem based upon a typographical error. About a dozen of these errors I have counted which are of the distressing kind; that is, they pervert the sense or confound the reader. Still I do

not pretend that this was the only thing that ailed the
poem; after all, it was a much better printed book
than Shakespeare's First Folio, which has not failed
to make its way in the world.

The reader will now understand why I have long de-
sired to give to this child of my brain a new dress.
The whole work has been revised, the old misprints
have been corrected, fresh errors have been guarded
against by a due outlay of patience and care, and
specially by a change of proof-reader. In addition,
quite a number of alterations have been made,
which, it is hoped, are improvements, being the result
of friendly suggestion and gathered experience from
many sources. Still there has been no attempt to re-
write the book or essentially modify it; to cleanse the
channel of certain impurities, not to change the direction of the stream has been the object.

Another reason for its publication at the present
time I may take the privilege of mentioning. It has
its place in a series of works, which are now to be col-
lected and printed, and which seek to embody the
spirit of Hellenism as it unfolds in the life of an individual and in the life of a period. The book presents a
phase of Greek antiquity transforming itself into the
modern world and into a modern experience. Many
such transformations have been recorded since the
antique ages; wonderful indeed is the capacity of the
Greek soul for re-incarnation. Its earliest philoso-
pher, Pythagoras, divined the deepest truth of it
and the most lasting. It has always to be born again,
having its great and its little epochs. Such a period
may be called a Renascence, though the limits of its
influence be very small, though it be confined to one
individual.

But whatever be the view concerning the met-
empsychosis of the Hellenic soul, rising and assum-
ing new shapes in the ages, one thing I may affirm
as certain: the present book is a link in the chain
which runs through and holds together the spiritual
activity of an individual life. The time has arrived

for bringing this entire chain to light in a series of printed books, each of which, independent in itself, is yet interlinked with the rest.

As I now look back at the writing of this poem, there comes to mind a little story connected with its origin, and with its relation to myself through a number of years, which story may help illuminate certain points in it, and possibly the whole work.

PERSONAL.

It may be taken for granted that the friends of an author wish to hear something of the history, inner and outer, of his book. Such a history may have as great value as the book itself. Criticism is becoming more and more an insight into development rather than a judgment, and development takes the author himself into account along with his work.

I do not remember the exact time when the story of Iphigenia began to exert an influence upon me. But I am certain that the first strong impression came through reading Goethe's *Iphigenia at Tauris* many years ago. That poem on several lines opens the eyes of the lover of the Hellenic spirit, not simply by virtue of its poetic merit but through the example it gives of the transfusion of the antique into the modern. It is old, yet it is new; it is not an imitation or reproduction of some ancient classic model, it is original in the best sense, being a true literary evolution.

Its influence must have been considerable, probably more than I was conscious of, since that influence was noticed and pointed out in a local periodical by Dr. W. T. Harris, then Superintendent of the Public Schools of St. Louis, in a review of *Clarence*, a dramatic poem written by me, during the years 1866-8, and printed some years later in a magazine. Still, I think that Goethe's poem impressed me then far more through its literary beauty, than through its treatment of the legend. Of course the character of Iphigenia, as there portrayed, I felt to be the central power of the poet's work, and her spiritual picture stayed with me.

IPHIGENIA.

The time when the legend began to dawn upon me in its full sweep and significance, was during my visit to Greece. At Aulis, where Iphigenia was sacrificed that the Greek fleet might sail and Helen be restored, the impression became overpowering; it rose into an intense, sympathetic emotion. The innocent maiden, then, must give herself for the guilty woman. The fact dawned clear upon my mind that the legend hinted, and to a degree prefigured the story of Christ, who also was sacrificed for a sinful world. At once the most diverse peoples seemed to be linked together in one great thought. So those old Greeks had this conception, which we usually call Christian; yet how different was their form of it! The great mediatorial figure at the heart of their story was, not a man, but a woman.

At Aulis the shape and the thought of Iphigenia crowded out everything else, as I now distinctly recollect, whenever I was alone. I rambled about the shore, I looked at the island in the bay, I went across to Chalcis; always I was in the atmosphere of the Greek maiden who gave herself as a sacrifice for the restoration of the lost woman. I stayed at Aulis, which is now a small Albanian village, nearly two days, mid a wild tumult of impressions; it was as if I had been present the whole time at the tragedy. Under such circumstances I began to see, in fact I was driven to see Iphigenia and Helen in their relation to each other. These two famous Greek women are counterparts, both are necessary to the one complete legend, to the one total cycle of man's spiritual history. It also became apparent that, in any adequate treatment of the legend, the two women must be brought together.

I now began to feel that Euripides, to whom we are chiefly indebted for our knowledge of Iphigenia, had not always grasped the true meaning of her story. The poet is naturally the best interpreter of the legend which his people have created. Such is, indeed, his highest function; what lies in a dim mythical form, and in many fragments of tales among men, he is to bring

to daylight and to put together, and then to stamp
with the image of beauty for all time. Euripides, in
spite of his excellences, is not as great as the legend
which he handles. To be sure, at the end of his
Iphigenia at Aulis he rises for once to the height of
the seer. But the call out of both his dramas on the
subject of Iphigenia is that the legend must be re-
written. That call has often been heard and answered
from the time of Euripides down to the present day.

Such was the step taken at Aulis in this experience
with Iphigenia. I had never before been wrought up
so intensely over a fiction; still this fiction, through all
time, has persisted as a fact more solid than granite.
Those who wish to see a longer account of Aulis, of its
scenery and impressions, can read it in the *Walk in
Hellas* (*Chapter Seventh*).

The further reflection came that this legend is still
in the process of evolution. It is not to be re-told to-
day in the old Greek sense, but in the modern sense.
The ancient conception must remain — it is eternal;
still it has been unfolding some 2,500 years and more,
into its true meaning, and it is not yet done unfolding.
It must be re-written again and again, with every new
age possibly, since the true legend is really as old as
man and develops with him.

Passing over the hills between Aulis and Delphi, on
foot and alone most of the way, but sometimes behind
the donkey with its master, I found pleasure in
giving the legend various shapes. Naturally I thought
of the dramatic form, which has dominated the story
from the beginning, doubtless from the overpowering
example of the three great Attic tragedians, all of whom
have had something to do with the subject of Iphigenia.
The action began to assume faint lines, and I think
it was at Thebes that I wrote out the first slight sketch
of an *Iphigenia at Aulis* as I sat in a wineshop, with
muleteers and drivers of cotton wagons noisily chatting
their modern Greek dialect about me, but in whose
speech I could catch many a word and many a turn of
expression which had come down from the time of old

Homer. Iphigenia, too, like the Greek tongue, must be modern yet ancient, and alive still in her sacrifice. Even the language she spoke became a living presence to me.

Arriving at Delphi, I found many other figures, historical and mythical, crowding into the vision along with that of Agamemnon's Daughter. She was thought of there, for the fact stands recorded; but I do not remember that the scheme of an *Iphigenia at Delphi* ever hovered before my mind during my somewhat protracted sojourn. The necessity of such an addition to the legend came later in my experience, though I must have already known that Goethe had planned a work of that name during his Italian journey.

Still in Delphi and in the Delphic region I absorbed the local scenery, and I felt the subtle connection which exists between the environment of nature and the great historical fact which has arisen in that environment. Delphi was once the spiritual center of the whole Hellenic race, which found its unity in the oracle, though never in a political organism. Delphi, therefore, gave the picture of the priestess, whose influence reached even barbaric peoples, and showed how a woman, doubtless with the aid of wise counselors, became for a time the grand mediatorial power of all Greece. The legend did not go beyond the fact lying before the eyes of every Greek, in the place which it gave to Iphigenia. To be sure the priestess was but the voice of the God who spoke through her; but to be such a voice and to hear the God when he speaks, is quite the highest gift of mortals.

The sojourn at Delphi having come to a close, I went to Corinth, and thence walked across the country to Mycenæ. The excavations of Schliemann had been concluded, most of the antiquities had been transported to Athens and elsewhere; but the great walls, the mountainous citadel, the Lions' Gate, the treasury of Atreus, and above all the landscape could not be carried off so easily; thus the best part of Mycenæ still remained. The place seemed to open a long vista back through antiquity to the time of Homer.

Again the image of Iphigenia appeared and began to flit through the ruins in company with Helen and other figures of the Trojan legend. What power was it that once sat on this hill? How does it come that around this spot gathers so much song and story?

Not only does the movement against Troy start from golden Mycenæ with its King Agamemnon as leader, but also the re-action against Helen, shadowed forth strongly in Greek tragedy, the ethical protest of the Greek mind against the career of the beautiful woman, seems to be located on this spot. Of that protest Iphigenia is the most important figure. Two opposing currents we see setting out from Mycenæ, yet both making one total movement.

The image of Iphigenia began to dominate me at Mycenæ as completely as it had previously at Aulis; she was greater than her father, and in certain ways she overtopped Helen even. I went with her to the citadel, climbed the mountain with her to the temple of Artemis; I followed in her company the brook plunging down through the gorge under the steep walls of the city; I plucked a flower in her garden and sat on her summer seat of rock in the shade which fell from an overhanging cliff.

Under these circumstances there grew up in my mind the conception of an *Iphigenia at Mycenæ*. It had to be the prelude of the two *Iphigenias* by Euripides. Evidently these plays pre-supposed something of the kind. Its three main facts became clear: it must bring together Iphigenia and Helen, Iphigenia and Paris, and then Helen and Paris. Thus all the elements which afterwards unfolded, were laid in the primal legend — the unfallen, the fallen and the tempter. That primal legend could well have existed, in its germ at least, at or before the time of Homer.

Accordingly, the story of *Iphigenia at Mycenæ*, began to spin itself out into many details, under that clear Greek sky with the view of mountain, plain and sea ever in the eye. It became to me a necessary stage in the development of the entire Trojan mythus. But there was no *Iphigenia at Mycenæ*, ancient or modern, that I ever heard of; so it had to be made. The myth-maker has still to-day his place, and has the right to weave his fabric anew. But I have no doubt that some old story-teller has already told this tale thousands of years ago, and I believe that some learned man will yet dig it out of the dust of an old library. Thus the three *Iphigenias* — at Mycenæ, at Aulis and at Tauris, began to shape themselves, in a crude chaotic way into a Trilogy, which still persisted in taking a dramatic form.

Another fact soon rose into prominence. The total cycle of the legend would not be complete, unless Iphigenia were brought back to Hellas for some purpose which would make her return a necessity, and which would show her in a new career. The old legend simply restored her to her land, and gave her a priesthood. But what is the inner ground of this return, in Greece itself? Then what locality is the best setting for her activity? Athens was thought of, as hinted by Euripides in one passage, but this poet leaves her finally at Brauron, an insignificant place in Attica. In Argos, in Sparta, and in other lands of Greece, legend pointed out some temple in which Iphigenia was declared to have served after her return from Tauris. Athens, truly the intellectual light of Hellas, had strong claims upon the new priesthood, but Delphi was manifestly the best place, as the recognized spiritual center of all Greece.

It was in Athens, whither I went after my visit at Mycenæ, that the whole scheme was sketched in its four parts, and each of these parts named from the place of the action. Four Iphigenias had arisen, or four phases of one great character in its spiritual process. But I could not then proceed with the work, it reached out beyond me. There was nothing to be done with it but to let it lie in the soul and unfold in its own time. I retraced my steps through Europe, and came back to America, in the year 1879; still the legend kept fermenting within me, trying to shape itself without success. Several times in the following years I re-wrote the scheme with new additions and sketched some scenes, but I was not ready; the work lay seething often, but formless.

At last a change came. Certain ups and downs of life in the years 1881–2, made me see and feel in myself what was wanted. Without something of an Iphigenia experience you cannot write an Iphigenia poem. You must be immolated by your own people, and you must consent to the sacrifice; you must leave home and go the way of the wanderer, who in exile must still keep the sacred fire burning in himself and in the world. Such is the great trial of life, be the stage small or large, be it in secret or in public. That inner ordeal by fire, the final test of character as well as of vocation, comes at last to every mortal.

The career of Iphigenia now became not only a living thing, but a personal experience, which rapidly shaped itself not out of fancy but out of life. It could no longer make a classic poem, but a romantic one in the Christian spirit. Such had been the development of this legend in history, such too its development in an individual. Form, meter, and treatment rose into clearness. Goethe and Racine had dropped the ancient chorus, but retained the dramatic form. But the dramatic form was now dropped, and the rhymed romantic epopee took its place. Thus the legend went back to Homer in its epical treatment, but came down to the modern world for the manner and the internal spirit. I ought to add that Lang's *Helen of Troy* furnished me with metrical hints of importance.

In the fall of 1882, the first Canto was begun and completed. In the course of the following winter it was read to various small literary circles in the West. The criticism was courteous and friendly, but through all the pleasant words I then felt, what I have often felt since, that the poem was going to mean to but few people what it meant to me. Within the next two

years the whole work was finished, and the four Iphigenias, yet one, stood before me at least, in word and
deed. I had lived the poem inwardly, and even out-
wardly to a certain extent. The various portions of
the work were written in my wanderings to widely
separated places: Avondale, Ohio; Concord, Mass.;
New York City; Terre Haute, Ind.; Peak's Island,
Maine. There can be no doubt that I had my reward
for this fidelity to Iphigenia.

Printed and given to the world, the work was no
longer mine individually, but anybody's. Six years
and more have gone by since its publication; I now
(summer of 1891) turn back to it almost as if it were
another man's production. I have not only revised the
text, but have again thought over the legend and read
its most important literary manifestations. I can say
that once more I have taken it up into my being and
let it flow through my daily life. This second working-
over, doubtless my last, of the Iphigenia legend I pro-
pose to add as a small pendant in prose, to the story in
verse. It is more than likely that some may be induced
to read the prose who would skip the verse. The main
object is to see the whole sweep of the legend, in its
germinal meaning, in its growth, and in its literary
manifestations.

THE IPHIGENIA LEGEND.

The great fact which gives to the Iphigenia legend
its deathless charm and interest, as well as its infinite
suggestiveness, is its similarity to the story of Christ.
There is in both the innocent sacrifice for another's
guilt; the sinless one must give himself that the sinful
one be redeemed and restored, and the act must be
voluntary. An awful thought it is, not to be enter-
tained in its reality without a shudder. There is, then,
another law besides justice in the government of this
universe. The human being, in his supreme grandeur,
is immolated by his people, and he accepts his sacrifice as a necessity of the world's order.

Yet the compensation must never be forgotten: by giving himself he saves himself. " He that loseth his life shall find it " is as true of Christ himself as of any of his followers. He had not been what he was, if he had not given himself. Christ himself was saved by his own sacrifice. Listen now to the heathen poet, Euripides. In the very pinch of agony the mother of Iphigenia cries out to her daughter who has resolved to give herself to the Goddess: "Having lost thee, my child " — " But thou shalt not lose me, I am saved," was the answer. (*Iph. at Aulis,* l. 1440.) Through her death has come salvation.

Another point of similarity which reaches deep into the divine order of things, is the missionary character common to both lives. " Go ye into all the world," is the strong command of the one, and the touchstone of his spirit. Iphigenia is carried to Tauris, the land of the Barbarians, where she serves as a priestess, and becomes the embodiment there, as well as the doctrine, of her own sacrifice. For the one, the limit of Jew and Gentile is broken down; for the other the limit of Greek and Barbarian is transcended; both are universal, and seek the transformation of humanity into the image of what is universal. That is the best solution of the problem of evil which has yet been reached.

Still the differences between the two lives are very marked and very important. In the one case the mediator is a woman, in the other case a man. The one belongs to the Occident, and has a subtle connection with its spirit; the other belongs to the Orient, and never loses his Hebrew features amid his universality. In the one case it is rather the secular, institutional life of man which is to be redeemed — Family and State, and we may add, Civilization. Helen must be restored to husband and country, to Europe. In the other case, it is the religious life of man which is to be saved, without much regard being paid to the things of Cæsar; man is mediated with God, is rescued from his own destructive thought and deed, and is harmonized with the divine order. In the end, this

will embrace State and Family and Civilization. The
Greek legend shows its secular side in being rather
the source of art with its vision through the senses;
the Hebrew life shows its religious power by being the
source of worship, with its contemplation of the Divine
through the soul. Still both characters unite at last
in the spirit; secularity and religiosity become one in
humanity. Both stories reach down to a common element in all peoples and foster it, and appeal to it, for
their power and inspiration.

We may, therefore, affirm that of all the legends
which the old Greek world has handed down to us, the
legend of Iphigenia is the most completely prophetic,
and, hence, has within it the possibility of the most
complete unfolding into the modern world.

It hints the later movement of Christianity in the
spiritual conquest of Heathendom, and reaches with
its alluring suggestiveness down into the present; may
we not say, even into the future? This significance of
the legend is a development, not an analogy, not an
allegory; the legend unfolds with the race, and
images ever afresh what the race has realized. Later
poets new-model the old story; looking back on time
from their vantage-ground, they see this unfolding
and give to the legend the new meaning, which is,
however, but a development of the old.

There is another fact which belongs in this connection; the legend is the product of the people, not of
an individual. Usually, it is at first in a fragmentary
condition; there are many shreds of the one great story
floating about, as we can see in the case of the Trojan
war. Every new recital, being oral and the direct inspiration of the Muse, adds fresh touches; thus the
variations of the same tale among the people are often
many and great.

Still the legend is, at bottom, one, in all of its fragments. The unity is latent, in the idea; the variety is
manifest, in the appearance. As long as the legend
remains in the mouths of the people, it continues to be
fragmentary, yet perpetually growing, changing, de-

veloping. Two things are to be noted in the popular
legend: outer fragmentariness, inner oneness. In this
condition the poet takes it up; he seizes the fragments
and throws them into the furnace of his genius; the
slag falls away and the pure gold remains. It is the
poet who brings out to light this inner unity of the
legend, he organizes all the fragments into one central
life; in his hands they assume a form and are a totality.
It is always difficult to grasp this unity, being such an
elusive thing, an idea. Many people to-day can see
only the fragments of the Iliad, even after the work of
the poet who has unified them.

But, back of the poem, the unity of the legend,
though implicit, is to be also seen. Just as the people
is one, but composed of many fragments and divisions,
each of which is nevertheless some shred of itself, so
the legend, the product and image of the people's
spirit, is one, though made up of many fragments.
The Great Man, or Hero of the People is the one man
who is the best summary of them all, being reduced to
one personality. The great poem in like manner unites
all the fragments of legend into one complete legend;
thus it is all of them and itself too. A true poem does
not merely tell the stories over again, as they have been
handed down; it organizes them into a unity which is
its very soul, while they are the body.

Still, after the poem has been written, the legend
does not cease growing; it develops, as the people develops, as the world develops. Writing ought not to
stop growth and cannot. The written word though
much less pliable than the spoken word, is also in the
process. Hence after a lapse of time the poem with its
legend must be re-written, and made to reflect the new
time and the new spirit. The story of Helen will have
to be re-told with every great revival of human spirit,
mirroring the fresh outlook of the soul down the ages.
Homer's story of Helen will not become superannuated,
but reach a higher appreciation; still the story will
have to be re-written. So it has been in the past, so it
will continue to be. The same is true of the story of

Iphigenia, perhaps even truer, for her story has a deeper prophetic vein than that of Helen.

It is now worth our while to take a short survey of the history of the Iphigenia legend in its literary transformations. As already hinted, it has often been rewritten; it has woven its thread of light through all literature from the Greek downwards. A little tracing of that thread is helpful, it will show the story developing with the race.

HISTORY OF THE IPHIGENIA LEGEND.

Homer does not mention the Iphigenia legend. In a single passage (*Iliad* IX. 145) Agamemnon speaks of Iphianassa as one of his three daughters, who is at home, and whom Achilles can have in marriage, if he will only cease from his wrath. If this be the earlier Iphigenia, and such is doubtless the case, she has not been sacrificed at Aulis before the departure for Troy.

Still from the silence of Homer, we have no right to infer that the legend had not begun to exist in his time, nor even that he did not know of it. The fact is that Homer knew many legends to which he makes merely a passing allusion. It is quite probable also that he knew many which he does not mention. There is no valid reason, therefore, for saying, as is usually done, that the Iphigenia legend is post-Homeric. Unquestionably it unfolded into new shapes after the time of Homer; but the likelihood is that it had begun unfolding before his time, as was the case with the story of Helen. All these legends existed before, and after, and with Homer; they changed, they grew, as living things must change and grow.

In fact, the earliest form of the Iphigenia legend must have been a song in the epical fashion of Homer. The dramatic form, in which we first find this legend, is itself a growth out of the epic. In the Iphigenia dramas of Euripides, one may still trace certain primitive epical elements, such as the interference of Artemis and of Athena.

Still one must see that the general thought of the

Iphigenia legend is in Homer too, though not yet ex-
plicit. All the Greeks before Troy had to offer themselves in sacrifice, quitting home and country for war,
that Helen be restored. Wives and children of the absent soldiers had to suffer, even to perish in the same
cause. But the vivid concentration of this thought
into a person, and a woman, too, is not the work of
Homer, but is first found in Æschylus, though he may
have derived it from the popular legend or from the
later epics. The dramatic character now steps forth,
living, acting with a principle in the heart.

Æschylus has transmitted to us the name of Iphigenia, and has spoken of her sacrifice at Aulis. She
does not appear in person in any of his extant dramas;
still she has taken her place in the legend, and Clytemnestra, in the *Agamemnon*, makes the sacrifice of
her daughter the chief motive or pretext for slaying
her own husband.

The second great tragic poet of Hellas, Sophocles,
also makes an allusion to the sacrifice of Iphigenia at
Aulis in his *Electra*. He too is said to have written
on the same subject a play which is lost. Both
Æschylus and Sophocles apparently think that
Iphigenia perished at Aulis, that she was not rescued
by any divine interference of the Goddess Artemis.
To be sure, from their silence we cannot infer that the
legend was altogether silent upon this point in their
day. It is, however, the third great tragic poet of
Greece, Euripides, who has given the fullest elabora-
tion of the Iphigenia legend. He has devoted two
plays to the subject, which are still extant, and which
have been the main source whence later dramatists
have drawn their materials.

The student of this legend will of necessity give to
these plays of Euripides a careful examination. They
are deeply suggestive though not always profoundly
treated. On the whole we have to conclude that the
legend is greater than the poet. These productions
were effective dramas, doubtless; they justify the
title of Euripides as being " the most tragic of poets ; "

still in many respects they must have seemed external
to the best Greek minds of the age of Socrates and
Plato — that is, of the poet's own age.

The Iphigenia legend has an historical importance
from the fact that it has mirrored itself in so many
souls of succeeding epochs, especially among Latin
peoples. In old Rome, Italy, France, it has had a
numerous offspring. But the greatest child of the
Iphigenia legend is of Teutonic origin. The poem of
Goethe may be called the best embodiment of the
spirit of the Iphigenia legend that has ever been
caught and held in human speech, whether in ancient
or modern times. Still the other efforts give some reflection of the age and nation of their authors. Thus
we have an image of Universal History cast into these
manifold transformations of a single old legend.

But we shall have to make a selection, and give a
short account of the four which have shown themselves
the most lasting and important, two of which belong to
antiquity and two to our modern epoch. They are
the *Iphigenia at Aulis*, as treated by Euripides and
Racine, and the *Iphigenia at Tauris* as treated by
Euripides and Goethe. This will be sufficient to show
the historic unfolding of the legend in the hands of its
greatest expositors.

Iphigenia at Aulis by Euripides.— The argument of
the play runs in this wise: The Greeks are detained
at Aulis by stress of weather; Calchas the sooth-sayer
declares that they never will reach Troy till Iphigenia,
the daughter of Agamemnon, be sacrificed to Artemis.
This is the stern background of the action; a priest's
declaration of the will of deity, which here demands
the slaughter of the innocent for the guilty.

Agamemnon sends for his daughter under pretext of
a marriage with Achilles, then repents; Menelaus also
urges the sacrifice at first, then he too repents, seeing
the tears of his brother. Meantime Iphigenia arrives
with her mother, Clytemnestra, to celebrate the marriage when the real situation is discovered. The
mother and Achilles seek to thwart the sacrifice.

Particularly Clytemnestra enforces the moral aspect of such a deed: "A pretty custom, forsooth, that children must pay the price of a bad woman," and "Menelaus obtain his Helen." Moreover Helen has a daughter, Hermione, and justice demands that this daughter be sacrificed instead of the daughter of the unoffending mother. "I, the faithful wife, shall be bereaved of my child, but she who has sinned, bearing her daughter under her care to Sparta, will be happy." Thus Clytemnestra strongly utters the moral protest against the claim of religion.

In contrast to this opposition of the mother, Iphigenia rises to her supreme height of character. After some hesitation, and even resistance, she yields and offers herself voluntarily. As her spirit grows clearer with the vision of her deed, she is not only ready, but is determined to die. "Hear me, mother, thinking upon what has entered my mind: I have determined to die, and this I would fain do gloriously, dismissing all ignoble thoughts." How far does her glance reach beyond that of her mother, who could only see in this sacrifice that Menelaus would recover his bad wife! But Iphigenia knows that her deed is "for the woman hereafter;" she beholds it in its universal aspect; "barbarians will no longer carry off Greek women," after the destruction of Troy, which she brings about through her sacrifice. The Greeks will sail and avenge the wrong of Helen whom Paris carried away. She declares that life is not the highest good: "It is not right that I should be too fond of life, for thou, O mother, hast brought me forth for the common good of Greece, not for thyself only."

There is, now and then, a hint of universal redemption running through her utterances: "All these things I, dying, shall redeem and my memory, for that I have freed Greece, will be blessed." In her vision of the future, she beholds herself in the center of the great Trojan enterprise: "I give my body for Greece; sacrifice it and take Troy. For a long time to come this will be my monument; this will be my children, my

marriage, my glory." Not much beyond this point
is it possible for the human soul to climb.

Yet Iphigenia mounts a step higher. Is this sacrifice really death? The mother speaks to her: "Having lost thee my child" — "But thou shalt not lose
me, I am saved." Sacrifice, then, is not death, but
life. Bad would it be for her, if she did not offer herself; then she were truly dead, buried in a living
tomb of flesh. Moreover the mother too will not fail
of the blessing: "Thou wilt be glorious, as far as I am
concerned."

Accordingly, there are to be no signs of mourning
for her death ; no tears, no cropping of the locks, no
wearing of dark garments. For does she not really
attain true life by her act? Finally she asks to be led
forth, not as a victim but as a conqueress: "Raise
the pæan, let the joyful song go forth to the Greeks ;
conduct me hence, the conqueror of the cities of Troy
and of the Phrygians." Then the parting word:
"Farewell, beloved light."

There can be no doubt that this character of
Iphigenia is conceived and expressed by the poet
in the supreme height of the spirit. She becomes
truly inspired in her sacrifice, a seeress. She fore-
shadows much that is to be unfolded afterwards, she
has the prophetic character. Hers is that wonderful
union of vision and the deed, which produces the
greatest figures of history and poetry. In this respect
no poet after Euripides has surpassed him, and in his
other play on Iphigenia he has by no means equaled
himself, as he shines forth here.

There is another trait of Iphigenia, which is also
found in the present drama: it is the nun-like element
in her character, which looks away from domestic life
to some universal end. She says, speaking of her
sacrifice: "this will be my marriage, my children, my
glory." The woman thus surrenders her life in the
Family, for a purpose which she deems above the
Family. This trait, already brought out by Euripides,

and inherent in the story, will be kept and intensified as the legend develops in the ages afterwards.

From a purely dramatic point of view, the play must be called effective. It has not only unity, but a strong vital center of action, namely the sacrifice, which is announced at the beginning and continues the main thing to the end. All the characters stand in some relation to this deed, mainly in an attitude of protest and horror. Agamemnon at first consents to it, then repents, and finally yields to what he deems a divine necessity. Menelaus is urgent at the start, then he, too, changes. The old messenger, Achilles, Clytemnestra, all stand in persistent hostility to this terrible demand for a human life.

Two rise up on the other side, hard as granite and high as heaven — the Goddess and the Priest. There is no reason given in this play for the dire command of the deity, though the poet elsewhere has hinted the ground of divine wrath. Thus the action shows the strong protest of humanity against the external authority of religion. Euripides feels and portrays the conflict of the new spirit with the old creed which has become a horrible superstition.

Still, in the end, the Goddess rescues the maiden who has so nobly offered herself in sacrifice, and the audience is, to a certain extent, reconciled with the divine order. Behind this gross fabric of superstition there is a power that saves. Instead of the human being, a stag lies bleeding on the altar, and Iphigenia has disappeared. This rescue is purely external in the way in which it is brought about, still we connect it with the voluntary deed of the maiden, who has really saved herself by her sacrifice.

Deeper than the protest of the ethical consciousness against a bloody religious rite is the reconciliation with religion in this play. Deity saves through self-sacrifice — that is the law which we can read here. It is not a tragedy exactly, it is a tragedy mediated in the deepest manner, and a woman is the grand mediatorial character. It touches at this point a whole series of

Shakespeare's plays usually classed as comedies, but by no means mirth provoking. Nay, it hints the Margaret who is saved in her self-surrender and death at the end of the first part of *Faust*.

So we must give Euripides credit for his character of Iphigenia in the latter part of this play. One thinks that he must have obtained his inspiration for such a high strain from Æschylus, who also treated this portion of the Iphigenia legend in a lost drama. Still the command of the Goddess at the beginning and at the end of the play is external and capricious; we cannot help feeling that the legend has something in it greater than the present dramatic presentation of it by Euripides. Before his time, some spirit, be it that of the people, or that of a poet, or both together, had drawn the vast outlines of the legend, which the later dramatist was not able to fill.

Iphigenia at Aulis by Racine. — The French poet, in his drama, also finds a substitute for Iphigenia at the altar; not the stag, but another woman. That is, Iphigenia is not sacrificed, she escapes by a contrivance of the dramatist. Thus she is no longer Iphigenia, the soul of her character is gone. The deep reconciliation, which comes through the sacrifice, is totally lost; she cannot now be saved through her grand self-immolation. The Christian poet falls infinitely behind the Heathen poet just in the spirit of Christianity.

Racine retains the same rigid background of a religious injunction which we find in Euripides. The command of the Goddess, enforced by the priest, is given to Agamemnon, who is to obey without question, though he knows no ground for such a terrible mandate. A passage declares that Calchas now is commander, a priest has usurped the authority of the King. One can feel here an allusion to France, possibly the unconscious background it is to Louis the Fourteenth and priestly domination.

But in this hard outer setting of a religious rite Racine spins a love story, Achilles being the lover of

Iphigenia. In order to make the plot more compli-
cated, there is introduced another woman, a character
unknown to Euripides. This new woman loves
Achilles; Eriphile is her name, and the two women
have their mutual jealousies, their secret cabals, and
also their open quarrel over their lover. Such has become our Greek nun in the hands of that good French-
man, Racine, who, it is said, could never see a novice
taking the veil without weeping. The details of the
Parisian love intrigue have a strange color when inter-
woven into the Greek fable.

In the last pinch of danger the heroic Achilles with
true gallantry resolves to rescue his lady-love from the
sacrificial altar by violence. This brings about the
solution. Eriphile, the hateful rival is really meant by
the Goddess, she being the daughter of Helen by
Theseus, and having been brought up in Lesbos, from
which island she has been taken captive in a maraud-
ing expedition of the Greeks. The confusion all arose
from the fact that she went under the name of Iphigenia; hence the Goddess meant one person, while the
Greeks thought she meant another. Calchas at the end
of the play corrects the mistake, which was his own,
and poor Eriphile, whom we are to hate, has to bleed.

So Racine has discovered a substitute for Iphigenia,
and he takes a good deal of credit to himself, in the
preface of his play, for his discovery. He has found
in classic authors (Stesichorus and Pausanias) authority for stating that it was Iphigenia, the daughter of
Helen, who was sacrificed at Aulis. He has entirely
lost sight of the sacrifice of the good for the bad,
whereby not only the bad is restored but even the good
is saved. But Eriphile too is innocent, though she be
the daughter of the sinful Helen, and though the poet
tries to make her hateful, so that it is hard to see what
Racine, from his own point of view, has gained. By
his way of saving, Iphigenia is certainly destroyed.
It is true that she personally offers herself, when there
is no need, for she is not taken.

Eriphile at the final moment, kills herself in a frenzy

of wrathful defiance; she is not slain by the priest,
nor does the Goddess interfere on her behalf. Thus
Racine thinks that he has gotten rid of an incredible
piece of superstition. The godlike element in his
work he has indeed gotten rid of. Now there is no
reconciliation with the command of the Goddess; it is
left a cruel arbitrary act of the deity without any saving power.

The play of Racine, to the taste of the present time
among English-speaking and German-speaking peoples,
turns to an unconscious parody of the Classic. How
Frenchy it all is, we cry out, particularly at the love intrigue. Still there is a side on which he was right in
principle; it is the manner of his execution to which we
cannot assent. He had the right to put his own time
into the legend. But he has not unfolded either the
legend or the character of Iphigenia into its true
modern life. He has also thrown into his play something which is discordant with the old story. In general the charge against him, is, that he has not
harmonized us with the Gods, but left us in a far
deeper discord with the divine order than the Heathen
poet did. He has solved the sacrifice of Iphigenia by
putting in her place a substitute, and an innocent
one at that. Whereat we cry out still, why sacrifice this
guiltless being? We refuse to accept the substitute,
and the Goddess does not save her; thus we are dropped at the end into utter discord.

It is clear that Racine in his desire to save "that
amiable and virtuous princess" has lost her soul. For
Iphigenia is mediated through her own sacrifice, not
through that of a substitute. Thus she becomes an
exemplar, since every human being is to bear manfully
his burden and not to put it upon another. In spite
of himself Racine turns our sympathy toward the poor
outcast Eriphile, who is the child of adverse fate, without any fault of her own.

Whatever be the exceptions which are now taken to
the play of Racine, it has met in times past with extraordinary favor. Voltaire has called it the tragedy

of all ages and of all nations, which is as near to per-
fection as human effort can be. Undoubtedly it has
dramatic movement; it has a skillful evolution of a
plot; it has minor situations which are effective; it
has striking and even subtle reflections. But the
grand dramatic, or rather, poetic problem of all times
and of all peoples, the reconciliation of man with the
divine order of the world, is not illuminated but dark-
ened by the play; the providential plan of the deity
stands above the poor mortal, like an iron heaven, which
may fall at any moment and crush him. Was not this
the French consciousness of the time of Louis the
Fourteenth? Arbitrary power with absolute submis-
sion of the individual is the supreme law both in
church and state. So Racine mirrored his own period,
which for us is happily past, and which in itself was
but a fleeting and not an eternal phase of the
ages.

What we now demand is a true unfolding of the
legend into modern life, yet with its universal thought
of reconciliation. First of all, we must have some
valid reason for that command of the Goddess, by
which the father is to sacrifice the daughter. Agamemnon must have done some guilty act, which is thus
to be expiated. The old legend gave several grounds,
all of them insufficient, it is true, for the wrath of
Artemis, the Goddess of purity, against the leader of
the Greeks. Even the deity must not be arbitrary,
but rational, and the divine command is not to be external merely, but transparent to reason. Thus dramatic
art is truly a guide and an illumination.

In Iphigenia, we are to see that the sacrifice makes
her character, and the deed is her completion. To
substitute another person is really her death. Even
the rescue by the Goddess is not to be dispensed with,
but is to be made internal likewise, and thus transfigured into a spiritual act of liberty. The poet must
show that Iphigenia just through her sacrifice being
voluntary, is saved in the divine sense. If she had not
given her life willingly, then she had found no salva-

14

tion. And that life must be taken, else the offering
has no necessity.

Calchas, too, must be transformed. He is to be
not the mere mouth-piece of divine tyranny and
cruelty; he must be the interpreter of the God, and
explain unto men the divine oracles. A true priest is
also a seer. In like manner all the other characters,
while retaining their personal traits, are to be illuminated from the great central light. Achilles, as hero
and as lover, is to see what sacrifice means, especially
the sacrifice of Iphigenia. So all the host, when it
sets sail, is to feel her spirit in itself, that spirit of
sacrifice which the Trojan war demanded of every
true Greek. He too, though innocent, is to meet
death that the guilty one be restored.

I may have done scant justice to this play of Racine,
but after a repeated reading of it I feel the alien element still. Many parallels have been drawn between
the French and the Greek poet in their treatment of
the present theme. A French writer states that before
the time of La Harpe, these parallels gave the superi-
ority to Racine; but that recently, say during the last
hundred years, Euripides has had the preference. If
this statement be true, French criticism no longer sup-
ports the lofty claim made for this play by Voltaire.

The Iphigenia at Tauris by Euripides. — The following short abstract touches the main incidents: Iphigenia, who is now far away from Greece at
Tauris, on the shores of the Black Sea, and is
priestess there in the temple of Artemis, has had a
dream which she interprets as indicating the death
of her brother Orestes, to whom she will, accordingly, pay funeral rites. In the mean time, Orestes
with his friend Pylades has reached the coast of
Tauris, in obedience to an oracle of Apollo, who
has told him to bring back the sacred image of his
sister, which fell from heaven, to the land of the
Athenians, when he (Orestes) would be free of the
pursuit of the Furies. The two strangers are brought
into the presence of Iphigenia for sacrifice, as it is

the custom of the Taurians to immolate all strangers to their Goddess. After some conversation, and chiefly by means of a letter, Iphigenia and Orestes, sister and brother, come to know each other, and we have the scene of the recognition. Then follows the plan of escape for all three, as Iphigenia also longs to return to Hellas. She rejects the advice to kill the King, Thoas, but is ready to deceive him by using his superstitious faith. All three escape to the sea-coast with the image, and actually embark, when the stratagem is discovered, and is told to Thoas by a messenger. The King is on hand to seize them, when the ship is driven back to the shore by winds and currents. When all seems lost, Minerva appears, and commands Thoas to let the fugitives depart in peace for their own land and take with them the sacred image, which is to have a special temple at Attica, and Iphigenia is to be a priestess at Brauron in the land of " God-built Athens."

Dramatic life there is in this piece of Euripides and continuous movement. It has two leading points which will always strongly engage the interest of an audience. These are the recognition and the flight. The sister, as every spectator sees, is about to sacrifice unwittingly her own brother; will she find out who he is? This interest the poet has skillfully used and intensified, up to the point of recognition. The next matter is the escape of the three Greeks, and the success of the stratagem. This part is not so well handled as the previous one, still the interest does not droop. The least happy portion of the drama is the last, in which Minerva appears; this *Deus ex machina* seems unnecessary, as the fugitives had already escaped; still they are brought back, that the Goddess might appear.

Compared with *Iphigenia at Aulis* of the same author, this drama is a falling off. It has not the same unity in thought and construction. But above all, the character of Iphigenia is not maintained at the same height. Here she has not the spirit of sacrifice which

we beheld gleaming forth from her look and utterance
there ; still less does she show the spirit of her mission.
She has done little to tame and humanize the wild barbarians ; she still sacrifices human beings to the
Goddess, according to the old cruel customs of
savages ; she shows many indications of spite and
revenge against her father and others who had a share
in the doings at Aulis. She sighs, in the narrow spirit
of the Greek, to quit the barbarous land for Athens,
"a happy city." This is not the Iphigenia whom
we beheld in the glory of self-sacrifice at Aulis. If the
present play was written as a continuation of the
Iphigenia at Aulis, Euripides had lost, not so much his
dramatic, as his spiritual power, of which he possesses
at times a considerable spark, in spite of his skeptical
tendencies.

Notwithstanding these drawbacks, the story of the
drama is infinitely suggestive. Here again we feel that
the legend which is the creation of the people is far
greater and deeper than its poet. The Greek woman,
going as priestess to barbaric lands, is verily a
prophetic figure, and the prophecy is still being ful-
filled. She is the hint of the future illumination, she is
the germ of the teacher, missionary, bearer of light to
the dark places of the world. But Euripides did not
behold her and portray her in this transfigured shape,
though it lay in the legend, that half-articulate voice of
the people, which the poet is to endow with a complete
and beautiful utterance. Other points in the drama
are profoundly suggestive of the time that was then
coming and still has not wholly arrived. Iphigenia
finds that the stranger whom she is about to hand over
to death is her brother ; a wonderful experience lies in
that — nothing less than that every stranger may be
her brother, and she could catch from it a glimpse of
universal brotherhood. Even the interference of
Minerva, Goddess of Wisdom, who is to speak her
word to the barbarian Thoas with effect, has its suggestion, though here the divinity is purely external in
her authority. That which Thoas now does through

terror, will yet be done through conviction, and the Goddess will be inside the King as well as outside. In the present drama, accordingly, Euripides shows himself a skillful playwright, but not the far-glancing seer with his world-bearing words. Yet the legend seems to be calling for the poet who is also the seer. Many, in the course of time, have answered the call and have re-written this *Iphigenia at Tauris.* Of these answers, ancient and modern, none are at present heard by men with any distinctness, if we make one exception. Goethe, our last supreme poet, has told again the tale of *Iphigenia at Tauris* in dramatic form, and we may now make a short study of the legend as he has unfolded it.

Iphigenia at Tauris by Goethe. — The thought of this poem and the suggestion of it lay in the Spirit of the Time (in the *Zeitgeist*) as well as in the individual poet. In Goethe's boyhood (1757) a French *Iphigenia at Tauris* by Guymond de la Touche made an extraordinary sensation at Paris, the echo of which went through Germany. In 1779, the same year in which Goethe's first prose sketch was made, a musical *Iphigenia at Tauris* rang through Europe, in Gluck's glorious opera of this name. Even Racine had made a plan of an *Iphigenia at Tauris*, first published in 1747, in which the son of Thoas is the lover of Iphigenia, who was rescued at Aulis and borne to Tauris by pirates, and not by the Goddess Artemis. Thus Racine shows at the start the love intrigue and the abolition of the divine element. There was a struggle in the century to embody this great legend; Goethe, the poet of the age, felt the struggle, and wrought at the task for many years till he succeeded. But he, with the others, leans upon the old Greek, Euripides, and the main study is to trace the evolution of the ancient poem into the modern.

The first fact that comes up before the mind in this comparative view is that Goethe's *Iphigenia at Tauris* shows itself to be, in its external features, quite the same as that of Euripides. The setting is the same, both actions are placed at Tauris in a barbarous land. Then many incidents are common to the two dramas: the priesthood of the Greek woman, the arrival of her brother Orestes pursued by the Furies, the recognition, the scheme to escape to Hellas, the final departure. Then too, the characters have the same names for the most part, and the same external outlines in the two dramas.

Such is the similarity; now for the difference. In spirit two works could not be more unlike. Euripides is narrowly Greek, Goethe is universal. In the hands of the German poet, the Hellenic features are transmuted into those of humanity. Hellenism there is in Goethe's poem, but not that Hellenism which contemns the Barbarian with a provisional exclusiveness. The Hellenism of Goethe is that which has taken up and transformed the barbarous world. This is the wonderful poetic alchemy; Euripides is not equal to his legend; Goethe unfolds it into the modern age. Thus, while it is old, it is also new. This poetic transfiguration we shall try to trace in a few details.

In the first place, Tauris is no longer a particular spot merely: it means all Barbary, or the modern world, which Greek culture has helped to civilize. The poet calls himself a Barbarian in the *Roman Elegies*; he is now celebrating what the Hellenic spirit has done for him and for his race. Tauris, from the bleak inhospitable locality in the North, such as we find it in Euripides, is transfigured into a world.

In the second place the incidents become radiant with new meaning. The stay of Iphigenia is now not merely a separation, a banishment from home, but is a priestly work. She has tamed the savages, she has done away with human sacrifices. She has transformed the king and people. Orestes, too, is to receive spirtual help from her. The stealing of the image of Diana is changed into a taking of the priestess home, for she is the true image which is to be restored to Greece. In all these matters we behold a rich inner life develop out of what seemed only external

events. We also see an old legend with its dim in-
stincts and suggestions unfold into the clear transparent fullness of time. The poem must be perused
with this illumination of the inner light else it is dark
indeed.

In the third place, the characters show the same
transfigured spirit within. Iphigenia wishes to return
home it is true, but this is to be after her work is done,
after her second great sacrifice has been made. How
different from the Iphigenia of Euripides, as he portrays her at Tauris! In Goethe, she will not resort to
deception, she abandons Greek lying and cunning, and
tells all to Thoas. She is truly a priestly, consecrated
character. Thoas, the King, has been also transformed; then he is to master his love. This love of
the King for the priestess is an addition of Goethe's,
though it is said to be found in an old French drama
on the same subject, and may have been suggested by
Racine's sketch. Orestes, too, is transformed, he
finds that it is not the outer image of the Goddess which
he must take away, but Iphigenia herself. That is the
cure of his madness.

From many points of view Goethe's poem is worthy
of careful study. It shows the true treatment of a
great legend, making it unfold with time into all that
time has unfolded. Some have called it a pure specimen
of the antique, others have declared it to be a modern
poem with an ancient name. It is really both Greek and
Teutonic, old and new, an image of the spirit clothing
itself in classic and romantic art. If it were a mere
imitation or reproduction of a Greek drama, its value
would be small. Again it is said to lack dramatic life.
It is doubtless somewhat deficient in outer incident,
and its movement on the surface seems too tranquil;
but its wealth of inner experience is not easily ex-
hausted, and a continued activity of the spirit it has.
It is more a drama of the soul than of incident. We
may fairly say, it is the best embodiment of the Iphigenia legend.

Very naturally such a production was not under-

stood in its own time. It had to create its readers,
yes, to develop them with the years. It retained the
dramatic form, yet its relation to the stage was a matter
of doubt. Three hours of the theater cannot report a
development, which has required three thousand years.
The poem demands time, not for the scene to shift,
but for the soul to change. His friends in Italy, in
which classic land he gave to it the final form, and his
friends in Weimar, had not, as he very mildly hints,
any just appreciation of the work. It was clearly a
failure at the start. Fifteen years after its appearance,
it was acted for the first time, yet with a good many
modifications, which still indicated a lack of appreciation.

Thus Goethe's poem reflects a long chapter of the
world's history. But it also reflects a chapter of the
poet's own history. The development of the world
and the development of the world's poet mirror each
other. The poem was not of sudden conception and
execution ; it was itself a growth, a development of ten
or a dozen years. He first wrote it down in 1779,
though he had already been carrying it around with
himself and working it over in his mind for several
years. This first shape was in prose. He transformed
it into meter in Italy. The change corresponds to a
great change in the poet himself. The wild period of
Storm and Stress passes into the serene classicism of
the Italian period. Goethe himself was tamed by his
long stay with Iphigenia ; the modern Barbarian records
his own transformation. Even before this final reconstruction in Italy, the poem had several re-modelings,
no less than five according to Duentzer.

Still the return of Iphigenia to Greece must be given
a more developed form than even Goethe has given it.
She must be shown doing her work in her own country
as she has done it in Barbary, for she has an important career still at home. Thoas, too, Barbarian transformed, must not merely permit her to go back in a
passive sort of way ; he must send her back, must
actively restore her to her native land ; nay, he must

go himself to Greece, with arms in hand if necessary. That is, the actual restoration of Iphigenia to Hellas is the work of the Barbarian.

When Goethe wrote his *Iphigenia at Tauris*, time had not yet prepared this content for his poem ; the legend of the ages had not yet developed into the actual restoration of Iphigenia to Hellas through the Barbarian. But in the hundred years since the first publication of his poem, the eternal germ lying in that old story has marvelously unfolded anew, so that the whole legend must be re-written. The Greek Revolution, which took place in Goethe's old age, more than thirty years after the appearance of his poem, was a grand new act in the world-drama of Iphigenia ; the nations of Europe, Barbarians to the old Greeks, called Hellas back to life and freedom. And we must understand that it was not Christian Greece which roused the sympathy and strength of Europe (America too had a hand in the matter) but it was Heathen Greece, with its memories, with the feeling of gratitude for its culture. Other Christian peoples were quietly left under the Turkish yoke by Christian Europe, but Greece was set free.

One step further we may move at the present date. The Greek restoration through the Barbarians, has been going on in my own time. When I was in Greece a dozen years ago, there was no free Thessaly. Now, through the treaty of Berlin, the Greek limit has been extended northward into the region of the ancient home of the Hellenic Gods, Mount Olympus. After centuries of captivity Greece is gradually getting her own, by the aid of the European Powers ; restoration is indeed the great fact of her present history, and the watchword of her choicest spirits. And it is again that Barbarian, Thoas, who has not merely stood by and let Iphigenia restore herself, but who has helped her in the most decisive way, if not with arms in hand this time, at least with gleaming bayonets in the background.

DEVELOPMENT OF CHARACTERS.

It has already been indicated that the characters of the legend develop as well as the story itself, and take new spiritual attributes as these unfold in the ages. Not only the characters of the legend, but also those of the great works of art, and for that matter those of real life, are not of to-day nor of yesterday merely; they are the apparent gift of the moment of time in which they come to light, but in a deeper sense they are the products of all time, and have a spiritual lineage which runs back through the past, often traceable to the twilight of the race. Thus it is with the Iphigenia legend, its personages have had many literary incarnations, which can be followed historically, if not to their beginning in time, at least to their beginning in letters. We shall now give a little attention to its leading characters separately, and study each of them in its historic unfolding. Hitherto we have seen how the legend as a whole develops; at present we shall consider the history of its individuals, tracing it down from Homer to our own time, and even taking a glance into the future. The three main personages only will be considered — Iphigenia, Orestes, Thoas. The other characters, compared to these, are incidental and may be omitted.

Iphigenia. (1.) In Homer, the daughter of Agamemnon, Iphianassa, is not sacrificed at Aulis, but is at home during the Trojan War. Still there is a great sacrifice, both of Greek men and Greek women, taking place through that war; thus the germinal thought of the character lies already in Homer.

(2.) In Æschylus and Sophocles, Iphigenia appears, and is the first grand sacrifice, imaging all others. But she is an involuntary one, it would seem, and is not and cannot be rescued by the Goddess at Aulis.

(3.) In Euripides, she is not only a sacrifice, but rises to being a voluntary one. through her own character. A great and noble addition is this trait; then she is rescued by the Goddess, and taken to Barbary. But she is not seen to have any special mission there among the Barbarians.

(4.) In Goethe, she has the missionary spirit, she humanizes Barbary. She also exercises a healing influence over her brother, Orestes, who is pursued by the Furies.

(5.) In the future unfolding of the legend, the return of Iphigenia to Hellas must be fully set forth. Both Euripides and Goethe have this return, but they motive it on her part by a subjective longing to get back home, a kind of nostalgia. This is well enough as far as it goes; but we must also be shown that she has a mission in Greece too, that she is to save it as she has saved Barbary. Thus her return has a real objective ground, and is not simply her desire or caprice or home-sickness. Otherwise it were the higher thing to stay at Tauris and continue her work. It is true that Goethe has several hints which look in this direction, but they are not developed. One thinks that his *Iphigenia at Delphi*, had he ever written it, would have unfolded on these lines.

Orestes. (1.) In Homer, Orestes is simply mentioned as the son of Agamemnon, a boy at home, undeveloped. The Furies are also noticed in Homer, but in no connection with Orestes; they too are undeveloped.

(2.) In Æschylus, the next great poet, both Orestes and the Furies are developed with unsurpassed power, in the grand dramatic Trilogy, called the *Oresteia*, after the name of the hero. Orestes slays his mother who has slain his father, and he is pursued by the Furies for the deed. Then he is delivered by a decision of the court of Areiopagus at Athens, in which the Goddess Pallas Athena has the casting vote. Great and true and impressive is this solution, whereby institutional authority puts an end to private vengeance, or the need of it, on the one hand, and, on the other, puts an end to the pursuit of the Furies. There can be no doubt that Æschylus has written, in his *Oresteia*, one of the great world-poems, which embodies not merely poetry and characters, but an epochal moment of

Time, a turning-point in Aryan civilization. Still Æschylus springs directly from Homer, is a Greek unfolding of the first Greek poet. Thus he comes after Homer both in time and in magnitude.

In Sophocles also we find an Orestes portrayed in the drama called *Electra*, which shows changes from Æschylus, especially in the dramatic handling of the story, but there is no noteworthy development in the spirit of the legend.

(3.) In Euripides, Orestes again appears, still pursued by the Furies, a part of whom refused to acquiesce in the decision of the Areiopagus. Thus Euripides notices the solution of Æschylus, but does not fully accept it. That is, though the outer law may set free, the inner sense of guilt remains, and some of the Furies still hunt the man of sin. Therefore a new process of purification is laid upon Orestes by the oracle of Apollo: he must bring back the sacred image of the sister from Tauris to Greece. Deeply hintful is this command of the Oracle; but Euripides, in his *Iphigenia at Tauris*, is purely external in his treatment of the legend and loses the soul of the whole story; he makes no inner connection between this act of bringing back the sacred image, and the diseased spirit of the man who is thereby to be healed.

(4.) In Goethe also Orestes is pursued by the Furies, and comes into the presence of his sister, who has the power of soothing their attack. But the grand contribution of Goethe to the legend at this point is, that the external necessity of bringing off the sacred image falls away; the sacred image which is to be restored to Greece is the sister herself, with her twenty years of sacrifice, and not that rude Taurian block of wood. Thus the Teutonic poet, in a way not only beautiful but soul-illuminating, internalizes and truly interprets Euripides, or rather unfolds the old legend into its true significance. The ugly theft of the outer semblance of the Goddess from the Barbarians is wholly done away with, and banished forever from the legend, and the modern seer with impressive strength

and sweetness brings to light a great and deeply puri-
fying conception, which reaches up and touches the
heart of universal religion.

(5.) Yet beyond Goethe we must go. We must unfold into completeness what Orestes brought back in
his sister, of what spiritual disease she cures him, but
above all, in what way she is to be helpful to her country, and to cure it too. Orestes is not merely himself
but also Greece, which is harassed by the Furies and
Fates. But Iphigenia, through her life, has gotten rid
of the limit of Barbary ; this was a real Fate to ancient
Greece, which was destined to perish, at least as a nation, through the old Barbarians. She has also gotten
rid of the Furies, the vengeance which ever begets
vengeance, not simply in an external sense, but chiefly
in the bosom of the man who cherishes it. Thus there
is to be a priestly service of Iphigenia at Delphi, the
spiritual center of the Hellenic world.

Thoas. (1.) In Homer, we may note the first glimmer of the distinction between Greeks and Barbarians,
the latter being marked off in one passage by their
manner of speech. Still in this case it may have been
only one of the ruder Greek dialects. Very significant
is the fact that the earliest and greatest poet of the
Greeks hardly reveals that limit and prejudice of race,
which at last became hardened into Fate, into their
very destiny. Hence there can be no Thoas in Homer.

(2.) In Æschylus and Sophocles, the distinction between Greek and Barbarian has become developed ; in
fact, it is firmly fixed in the Greek national character, a limit which it will take ages to overcome, and
indeed a reconstruction of the world. It is the dark
demonic element which grew out of the struggle for
Greek freedom against the Persian. Æschylus and
Sophocles have no Iphigenia at Tauris, could not well
have in their time, and hence they have no Thoas, the
representative of the Barbarians. Still they have the
distinction.

(3.) In Euripides, Thoas first appears, the barbarous king of Barbarians, the embodiment of that great

outlying world to the North of Greece, not to the East as in Æschylus. Thoas is portrayed by Euripides, as cruel, superstitious, ignorant, in fine as the contrast to the beautiful and cultured Greek of Athens. But it is a wonderful step in the growth of the legend to see Barbary incarnated in one person.

(4.) In Goethe, Thoas has been humanized by the long stay of the Greek priestess. Thus he stands for the many ages of development which lie between the Hellenic and Teutonic poet, the latter of whom is now the Barbarian. Still Thoas has the danger of relapsing into savagery through disappointed love. But even this last sparkle of desire for the selfish possession of what is spiritual, is suppressed though not extinguished; his individual love is subdued if not reconciled by the priestess, and he permits her to return home in peace. Somewhat sullen perhaps, certainly cold and passive is that last word of his to the parting Iphigenia: "Farewell."

(5.) This character can be developed much beyond what we find in Goethe; indeed time has brought out such a development, as before said, since the appearance of Goethe's poem. Thoas, the Barbarian, must not merely suffer Iphigenia to return to Hellas, he must bring her back, he must go himself and help her in her new work. Then the historical measure of the legend will be filled up to date, and may voicelessly await its next grand epoch of expression. What she has done for him and his world, he must do for her and her world. The final restoration of Iphigenia to Hellas has been and is to be the work of Barbarians, yet with active co-operation on her part.

We are inclined to think that Goethe himself rubbed against the bounds of his present drama. In Italy, when he began to transform his earlier work, and re-think it all with the new experience, the conception of an *Iphigenia at Delphi* rose in his mind, as the completion of the legend. Hardly otherwise could it have been, for he is the limit-transcending seer as well as the limit-fixing poet of these modern days; what stirs him temporarily, often has a far-reaching significance prophetic of worlds yet to rise. He never completed even a full scheme of the new drama; he had too much other work partially finished, which called for completion. So he resolutely brought to an end his *Iphigenia at Tauris*, which was already written in prose, and left his unfinished idea to the future.

Besides these three characters — Iphigenia, Orestes, Thoas — there are some minor characters, like Calchas and Pylades, which might be developed on the same historical lines. Calchas would show the priestly function of the man developing from the old to the new, though that function is seen in its highest power in the woman of the legend, Iphigenia. Pylades would reveal the conception of friendship, as it unfolds from the ancient view into that of our own era. In fact, some dramas in antiquity (as the *Dulorestes*) and some in modern times (several on the French stage) have made the friendship of Orestes and Pylades the center of the dramatic interest. Such a poetic treatment, however, does not embrace the universal sweep of the legend, but simply follows out one of its subordinate branches.

Still the main interest and value of the study of the Iphigenia legend is to behold the whole of it from beginning to end, in all the forms which it has taken through time, and to see it unfolding with the race and mirroring the entire course of civilization. Thus the eye and the soul become opened to the grand significance of the legend in the education of mankind, especially of infant mankind; we see too that it marks out the path and the sweep of the world's literature; it bears also the suggestion, if not the doctrine, of an universal religion. Such a legend truly teaches spiritual development, with its twofold correspondence in the race and in the individual, as the grand fact of the world's history. Shall we not say that the movement of humanity is imaged together in legend, in literature, and in religion?

We must, indeed, sympathetically take up all manifestations into our spirit; we must feel that all the poems on the Iphigenia legend, all its incarnations, literary, musical, mythological, even philosophical and critical, are only single strains which blend together and make one vast orchestral harmony. Then we have reached a true appreciation of the Iphigenia legend.

But even thus we are not done. One legend only is ours, we must take others and trace them to a like completion. Many are these legendary treasures, the race has made them and preserved them, for the popular consciousness is at bottom mythical. We shall find every true legend — by this is meant not a mere sport of fancy or ingenious fabrication — has the history of man in it, wholly or in part, and has the power of developing with man. Especially those legends which have flowered into great poems — that of the struggle between Orient and Occident in Homer, that of the Future State in Dante, that of Negation in Goethe's Faust, — are the chosen ones for study and contemplation, chosen by the world's greatest spirits and set to the music of the spheres.